A FAVOUR TOO FAR by A

CHAPTERS

CAN I DO THAT AGAIN?
THE AIRSHIP'S MAIDEN FLIGHT
HONG KONG
THE DRIVING TEST
THE NORFOLK BROADS
JURY SERVICE
POACHER TO GAMEKEEPER
MOBILE PHONES
TWO DRUNKS ON A COACH
CHICKEN, CHIPS and ENGINE OIL SIR?
POP GOES THE WEASEL

RAG 'n' BONE MAN

I was born at Upton Park in East Ham in war torn London within spitting distance of West Ham United football club's Boleyn Ground. East Ham is now known as Newham.

My maternal grandparents were Eliza and Tom, who lived in Boleyn Road which was adjacent to the Boleyn ground. I had three older brothers all of whom were raised nearby. Fred the eldest, John, David and finally me. My parents were Daisy and Sam. I will try to record facts chronologically but dates cannot be relied upon as strictly correct as memories become cloudy with age. I will however for historical reasons try as hard as possible to be accurate.

I have seen so many changes throughout my life and will try to record those which may be of interest to future generations. We must have moved to High Street South, East Ham when I was about 5 years old and I clearly recall there was a United Dairies Milk Depot opposite as I can remember the horse and carts leaving the depot early in the morning to start their milk rounds.

The next move was to a flat on the upper floors in Folkestone Road also in East Ham.

Mum was a home help (care worker in todays' parlance) and Dad a fitter in the local Power Station. He had been an aircraft mechanic in the Royal Air Force in the Second World War but never spoke about it. His generation just didn't. The war had only just finished when I was born and fortunately for everybody things were starting to get better.

I wouldn't have realised at the time but the people in the East End of London had suffered terribly because of the German bombing campaign. My early childhood had been spent in the many bomb sites close by, re-enacting the exploits of our brave forces. Grandad Tom was a rag and bone man and quite often would take me on his rounds on his horse and cart. In fact the earliest memory I have is of going over the cobblestone road which was Canning Town Bridge in those days.

I clearly remember him cursing the few cars that were on the roads then, as he would have been in trouble had he been late in picking up my gran who was a cleaner on the ships in the King George V and Albert docks. All long since gone and gentrified now with City airport in their midst.

I went to Gooseley Lane infant school but have very little memory of my time there. Ironically approximately 10 years later whilst boxing for Dagenham school boys, I returned in a boxing competition held in this school and had Ted 'kid' Lewis, a former world champion boxer as the second in my corner.

A great thrill at the time but sadly no photographs were taken, as in those days there were no 'i-phones, tablets etc.' If anybody had a camera it was very expensive to get the photos developed. Even had some been taken at the time, they would probably have been thrown out by my mother in later life when she developed dementia.

I have no photographs or mementos until I reached my late teens as everything from our childhoods were disposed of by Mum. My brothers' football medals were also thrown out. It wasn't her fault, she was ill. We didn't know then what we know now about dementia. The only memories I have of living in East Ham are not that clear but I do remember some with fondness. Father James Rolls, the vicar of St. Mary Magdelene's Church, at the junction of Becton Way (now the A13 road) and High Street South.

A real gentleman.

Both my brothers and I had been choir boys at his church. He was a great giver to charity and took many of us under privileged children on holidays. Generous in both pocket and heart. We all for years thought he was one of the Rolls Royce brothers who had withdrawn his money from the company to do work in his vocation.

Many years later I bumped into him and found him as warm and affable as I remembered him as a child.

I heard of his death with sorrow in my 40's and only then discovered that it was a myth about being a Rolls Royce brother but he was in fact a member of the Pearl Assurance family. Needless to say I understand he left his millions to charity upon his passing.

Silver three penny pieces.

These actually pre-dated the three penny pieces which were common currency until perhaps decimalisation. The silver ones were put into Christmas puddings and to find one in your pudding at Christmas was a rare luxury. They looked like the modern silver 5 pence piece. I say a rare luxury, especially when you consider I did and still do, hate Christmas pudding but I wasn't giving up on the chance of getting one by not having any '*afters*' following dinner. It wasn't known as 'lunch' to cockneys.

The Lemonade Man.

He used to deliver around the council estate in his lorry which had sloping sides, similar to those used by vans nowadays to carry large sheets of glass. There were ridges on the side to stop the wooden crates which held the glass bottles from dropping off. Multi-purpose plastic containers as such had not been invented then, it was glass or cans. They carried the normal flavours plus new ones to us, like dandelion and burdock. I think the name of the drinks company was Biddel and Gingel.

My other prominent memory was of being taken to the 'men only' barbers in Gooseley Lane by my dad. The barber or '*Hacker Len*' as he was known used to put a plank of wood across the hairdressers chair for the kids to sit on to enable him to cut hair without him having to bend over.

It always mystified me why the barber would ask all the dads when he had finished cutting their hair,

'Would they like anything for the weekend?'

He never asked the kids though! It was many years later before I realised it was a euphemism for 'did they want to buy any what we now call condoms?'

In those days I believe it was virtually the only place the working man could buy them discreetly, but I could be wrong.

GRANDAD'S YARD

I used to love sitting alongside grandad watching him gently prompting the horse to speed up or to slow down whenever somebody would bring out a bag of rags and try and negotiate with him to give them two plates instead of just the one.

He had been doing the rounds for too many years for anybody to try and con him into giving them more than their bag was actually worth.

It was just after the war and the East End of London had been straddled with bombs for so long that there were almost more bombsites than houses. As a young boy I had known of nothing else so it meant very little to me.

Everything was so drab that even my innocent eyes couldn't help but notice the greyness all around us. The lines full of washing seemed to have no colour and the whites didn't even look white.

Years of rationing and austerity had taken its toll on the ever resilient cockneys however gran and grandad managed to eke out a living from their respective jobs.

They lived in a terrace house in the bottom part of Boleyn road and the old 'Chicken Run Stand' of West Ham's then Boleyn ground was only yards away. One of my jobs at a very tender age was to put out beer crates and a '*No parking. Space needed for Horse*' sign in the road in front of the house to enable grandad to 'park' the horse and cart on return from his rounds.

On match days the road would frequently fill up with cars belonging to the fans going to watch the football. There was access at the back of the house leading to a stable in the garden allowing him to bed the horse down for the night but of a daytime he would take his wares through the front entrance, much to the annoyance of my gran.

I never recalled anybody ever removing the crates probably because of the thought of coming back to their cars to find a load of horse shit all over their pride and joy or even worse finding hoof marks all over the shiny metal.

He kept chickens and the occasional goat so there was no shortage of eggs or milk. Rags and other junk was piled up in the garden waiting to be sold on to the various clothes *'re-cycling'* yards that were abundant at the time.

I used the word garden loosely, as there was not a blade of grass to be seen. Vermin occasionally reared their ugly heads from under the piles of warm often soaked through cloth they called home but it didn't seem to bother anybody, not even the neighbours. Nowadays

Environmental Health Officers would have a season ticket to visit grandad's yard.

Different times.

My mum's spinster sister Susan or '*Aunt Sook*' as she was known to all the grandchildren lived with them. It was she who taught me how to sew and knit, not a talent I tended to boast about in later years when I started school as we all know kids can be very cruel and in those days it was best to be gender correct.

I am however eternally grateful for her patience in teaching me skills that have served me well throughout my life. Considering she had suffered with seizures throughout her life she never complained about anything.

I only experienced her having one seizure but by then I was a teenager and the effect was less traumatic than had I seen it as a very young boy.

It was a joy to see dad playfully tease her about only having them to avoid doing her chores. She would get quite embarrassed and mum would chide him to stop teasing her sister.

I have fond memories of her and kept in touch throughout her life.

As I recall she did most of the household chores of hand washing and cooking on a big old *aga*. There were no electric washing machines and even had there been there would have been no electric to power them.

The house only had gas lights which would be lit at dusk by means of a long tapered lighter igniting the gas mantles. As a very young boy it used to fascinate me to help '*Sook*' light them and watch the room slowly illuminate. Where we lived was modern and had electricity therefore gas lamps were a novelty to me.

Whilst all of the rooms had fireplaces the only room which was generally warm was the kitchen because the *aga* would be almost constantly on necessitating us spending most of our time there.

The other rooms were rarely lit or heated thus saving on costs. The whole house because of this was dreadfully dark and dismal. To a small boy this was scary and I rarely ventured from the kitchen and certainly not without an adult. It was like being in a haunted house to me.

It is now a lifetime away but I still recall as a young boy of about four or five years old grandad stopping off at the Wakefield Arms and tying the horse and cart up outside with me still on board.

He would go inside and come out a few minutes later with an arrowroot biscuit for me and a pail of water for the horse. We were then both left to our own devices until he had quenched his thirst.

The horse had negotiated the trip home so many times that it didn't really matter whether grandad was drunk or sober when he left the pub as he always managed to get him home safely.

When he was on his own apparently it wasn't unheard of on his return home for cries from the neighbours of 'He's pissed again Eliza and the horse doesn't look to sober either'.

Had he have got in such a state with me with him, he would never of heard the last of it from gran and mum. He had suffered their wrath on several occasions in the past when he had come home drunk with my older brothers on board.

I had so much fun with him as my brothers before me must have. He had been threatened by gran and mum many times to not let me place his bets with '*Nippy the bookie*' which I often asked him to let me do.

Gambling was illegal then and generally the only way a bet could be placed on horse or greyhound racing was via illegal bookmakers. The only real flutter allowed was on the football pools which for some incomprehensible reason wasn't considered to be gambling.

How the system worked was that the '*bookie*' would wait on a street corner at a pre-determined time known only to the locals and they in turn would approach him with their bets written on bits of paper and the money wrapped inside.

The '*bookies*' always tried to position themselves on street corners so they would have clear vision in all directions so that they could see if any police officers were approaching them.

Should that ever be the case they would have young fit lads stationed nearby to quickly take the betting slips off them and outrun the police. No betting slips, no evidence.

On the whole though this was rarely necessary as the police liked a bet as well and often placed a bet through third parties', so in general the '*bookies*' were left alone.

The gambling laws were archaic and in later years were to be abolished with the introduction of new Gaming regulations which subsequently brought in what we now know as betting shops.

'*Bookies*' who plied their trade on street corners were not the only way the working man could have a bet. Some shops, my uncle's being one of them, accepted bets under the counter.

Tom was my dad's sister Lucy's husband and she and Tom owned a small sweet shop in Forest Gate in the East End of London.

I loved my aunt Lucy to bits and not just because she had a sweet shop! It helped though. They had no children of their own and she would spoil me rotten. She was a very warm person and always gave me loads of hugs. Tom though was completely different.

He was the opposite of Lucy. It was always Lucy who would take me out front to the shop and let me choose as many sweets as I wanted whereas Tom would generally just bring me one sweet. A lolly or tube of lemonade sweets was the norm. I suppose he could best be described as Arkwright the Ronnie Barker character in 'Open all Hours.'

At the same time he could be hilarious with a very dry wit and I remember him having a dog which ate razor blades which was true but if ever he was asked why the dog did it Tom would say because he wouldn't let him have light bulbs because they were too expensive.

He wasn't a cold man, far from it but appeared to be in his own little world however he did teach me the basics of being a bookmaker.

The saying has always been '*you will never see a poor bookmaker as they are the only winners'*

Not Tom. You shouldn't have been a '*bookie*' if you didn't have a good memory and he certainly didn't. How it worked was that people would bring him their bets the same way as they would to a street corner '*bookie*'.

Tom didn't have young fit runners to help him should the police decide to take a look at him but what he did have unbeknownst to the police was a mother who owned the public house next door. As soon as bets were given to him Lucy immediately passed them to her via an adjoining door to the pub out of view of everybody.

Were they ever to be searched no betting slips would be found. No evidence, no prosecution.

I don't think they ever had a problem with the police as it was a very tight knit community and coppers would have been spotted a mile away.

Tom's downfall was his memory or lack of it. His customer's bets were generally small. For example in today's money a punter would put down a bet with him of £1 on a horse at odds of 3 to 1 thus if it won the punter would win £3 plus his £1 stake money back as well.

He could handle this with ease as he himself would make his money on all of the bets he had taken on the horses that hadn't won on that same race. The problems started if a punter wanted to put down £300 on the horse. If it lost Tom would have a tidy £300 in his pocket but if it won he would have to pay out £900 plus the £300 stake money.

All bookmakers do what is called '*laying off*'. As a generality Tom would spread the bet by putting a bet of £50 with each of 5 other bookmakers keeping only £50 of the bet for him thus '*laying off*' £250 of the liability should the horse win. Tom would still have to pay out £150 but that would be much more manageable than paying out £900 pounds on the full bet.

If it lost at least he would have made £50 as opposed to the £300 pounds had he not '*laid it off*' and with less of the risk.

This is only a crude example but as a rule works by limiting the liability however it obviously depends on remembering to '*lay off*' the bet. Unfortunately, Tom had a habit of being distracted by other customers whilst serving in the shop and forgot to '*lay off*' the large bets. Lucy would constantly admonish him but to no avail.

Later in life I was to discover that my son-in-law and his siblings lived in the next road to Tom and Lucy's shop and spent time in their childhood gorging on their extensive sweet selection.

I saw the shop through a child's eyes as being very large but with hindsight it was in fact probably quite pokey.

The shelves were always packed with glass jars full of sherbet lemons, aniseed balls, liquorice allsorts and many other varieties.

It was a great thrill when Lucy showed me how to weigh out the sweets and put them into paper bags for the waiting children who gazed at me with such envy. What child wouldn't want to be able to do that.

The dog hovered close to me as he knew I would drop some as I had great difficulty at times emptying them from the scales into the bags. Anything I dropped he would pounce upon. Tom would gently mock me saying that I must get it right otherwise I would make the dog vomit as he was only used to having razor blades in his diet.

For some reason and I don't know why, Tom always seemed to have gadgets in the living rooms behind the shop. There was the time he told us that we were about to see something very special that evening. He had he said, managed to get hold of a colour television. Now this was the 1950's and a decent picture on the black and white sets wasn't always possible so colour would have been out of the question.

He always considered himself to be a bit of a magician and often could be seen in the shop trying to entertain the kids with his magic. He was a bit like Tommy

Cooper without the talent however the kids seemed to enjoy it.

Being a child I naively waited with excitement to see the colour television but he couldn't show us this marvel until later in the evening when the shop became less busy. In fairness for such a small shop he did a roaring trade.

The final moment arrived for him to switch on the TV. Firstly though, he came from the back of the old lean-to with a piece of plastic about the same size as the screen. He stuck the plastic on the screen with tape and stood back to admire his handy-work. He seemed to be genuinely pleased with himself.

The set was switched on and about five minutes later a picture started to appear. In those days it would take that long for the tube to warm up.

WE HAD COLOUR!!

Well sort of if you looked at the screen through a child's eyes. The design of the plastic cover certainly produced colours. There was a vertical line of a sort of green, a sort of red and a sort of mauve. All being about one sixteenth of an inch thick.

I tried to look suitably impressed which was more than mum, dad and Lucy did.

He had after all produced colour but unfortunately there was no picture to be seen. Sounds of guns gave us a clue that it was a Western being shown.

It was the first and only time I heard Lucy swear.

'You have raised a little boy's hopes of seeing colour on the television and what have you produced?

Sweet sod all!

This was strong language for her. Dad was the same. Throughout his life I never heard him say anything stronger.

THE MOVE TO ESSEX

I can remember leaving Folkestone Road in the removal van and arriving with excitement in Dagenham but nothing about the actual journey or who was with me in the van.

Mum and dad travelled on the bus I think as we did not have a car like most other people didn't in those days. I think my other brothers were doing military service at the time.

This new place was a three bedroom house and had a garden. We had never had a garden before and I can remember pestering dad for ages to plant some vegetables, which he eventually did.

Dagenham at that time was like moving into the country for us, compared to the East End of London. Even on the first day I made friends with Johnny, Roy, Roger and Charlie who lived in the next street.

I can clearly remember on the same day them showing me where the local shops were at the Dagenham Heathway, a tube station on the District line. I must have been 8-9 years old and I quickly settled into Thomas Arnold junior boy's school which was in the next road.

Some years later, unbeknownst to me, Maria, my youngest daughter Caron's oldest friend, informed me that she attended the same school a generation later and by then it had obviously become a mixed school.

I spent the next couple of years playing football in the street with my mates. There was hardly ever a car in the road, so it was quite safe.

We just did what boys of my age did at the time, exploring the local area with new found friends and though I haven't seen most of them for about 60 years, I remember them all with fondness. Over the ensuing years I bumped into them all, until we lost touch in my early 20's.

THE 11 PLUS EXAM.

I was quite a bright kid in junior school and enjoyed learning. For some reason most of the rest of the boys considered that to be madness. To this day I have never understood why. They all seemed to be of the opinion that they were destined to go to the local secondary modern school. Grammar school didn't seem to be on the agenda for them.

We all had to sit the 11 plus exam but for some reason I was the only one in my year who passed first time. One other boy was allowed to re-sit the exam as he had achieved a near pass and subsequently passed and joined me in electing to go to Dagenham County High.

The downside then was that the legal school leaving age was 15, but at Grammar schools you had to stay until you were 16. I can't say I really enjoyed my time there but I also didn't hate it either. Believe it or not, even in Dagenham which in later years claimed notoriety as the most deprived area in '*London*', despite the fact it was actually in Essex, there was still a class system in the school. Many of the pupils were from middle class families who were bussed in from Romford, Hornchurch and Gidea Park, much more affluent areas at the time.

The one thing I did detest was the fact that Dudley Moore, a former pupil of the school and at that time at Cambridge University, was constantly drummed into us as an inspiration. He obviously wasn't famous then and I can honestly say in fairness to most of the other students, that they were also fed up of being frequently updated on his achievements.

In his defence he did not ask for the idolatry and went on to become one of our most famous musicians and comedians. His double acts with Peter Cook are now legendary.

There was however one incident I do remember at County High which caused me no end of embarrassment.

Back in the 1950's swimming trunks were generally made of wool and the variety of materials we now have to make clothing had either not then been invented or been too expensive to manufacture.

The whole school were taken by form order in the summer to a local lido for the purpose of teaching those pupils who couldn't swim the opportunity to learn and those that could swim were provided with a chance to get out in the fresh air and enjoy being away from the strict discipline of the classroom which was then the norm.

Unfortunately the wearing of wool swimming trunks was a bit hazardous. The wool quite naturally absorbed water and it was a gamble upon exiting the pool as to whether the weight of the absorbed water in the trunks would allow them to stay attached to your body.

As boys and girls attended the lessons together we relied upon '*a whistle and a prayer*' to keep our dignity intact. Most of us had to wear these monstrosities so we were all generally in the same boat. Only the more affluent kids had the luxury of wearing a pair made out of the newly emerging nylon type trunks or even had a flash belt to keep them up. The rest of us just had string to keep '*our bad boys'* inside our trunks.

At the time my brother John was serving in the British Army of the Rhine in Germany and for my birthday sent a pair of trunks made out of one of the new materials not yet available in this country. Ironic really seeing as we had supposedly won the War.

They were even made to look like they were made out of Ocelot skin. As any child knows even though they were different and very smart and the thought was well intentioned, it wasn't a good idea for any child to stand out from the crowd.

This fact was exacerbated by the fact that they were at least three times too big for me. Nevertheless mum had decided that I should wear them the next time the opportunity presented itself.

As she only packed this pair on swimming lesson day I had very little choice but to wear them. At least they had thin white cord to keep them up as opposed to the bits of string or metal snake buckled belts we had on the wool ones.

All very well on somebody they fitted properly but no matter how hard I tried to tighten the cord they would not keep stationary on my young thighs.

The only solution was to try and enter the water with one hand clutching on to them for dear life. Not an easy task I can assure you. Surprisingly though the physics of the new type of material seemed to make it grip my torso once in the water.

So far so good I thought. Not as bad as I had imagined until it was time to get out of the pool. As soon as I took a step onto dry land for some reason the tightness of the trunks on my skin disappeared and my confidence in being able to move by holding onto them with one hand was misplaced.

Before I had time to cover my dignity they were around my ankles.

My mates thought it hilarious and the girls weren't any less forgiving.

For weeks afterwards I took the brunt of every '*Willie*' joke that has ever existed. Blackboards whenever I entered a classroom had some juvenile attempt at a drawing of my genitals plastered all over them.

I wouldn't have minded but they weren't even very complimentary about the size. Considering sizes always looked the same after coming out of cold water I thought it most unfair.

I am sure that even the teachers were complicit in the drawings, as the time it must have taken the toe rags to do them couldn't have gone unnoticed.

On reflection I can now take some solace in the fact that camera phones had not been invented or some scumbag would undoubtedly have published on social media had it then been in existence. Bloody Ocelots!

BIKE MAD

It was the first summer after starting high school and my mates were still those I had known since the move to Dagenham.

I had made friends at my new school but relationships had not yet developed enough to spend the whole of the summer school holidays with them. It was different with my old friends as we had already bonded into a gang over the relatively few years I had known them.

A gang then was a million miles away from the sinister interpretation we now associate with the name. We were 12 year old kids who spent our days together travelling around the local area on our bikes having adventures, some real and some imaginary.

Our bikes were standard drop handles and although they hadn't been bought new we cherished them as if they had been. We spruced them up with badges and go faster stripes as if we were competitors in the Tour de France.

My brother John had re-sprayed his old car in a beautiful royal blue colour and with the paint he had left over he did my bike as well. I was the envy of the street as it looked a picture. I tried to be as humble as I could about it but it was difficult. It must have been plain to see I was really chuffed.

Roger, Johnny, Charlie and I vowed that summer to spread our wings and cycle out of our local area. We were after all now all at least 12 years old so hatched up a plan to go camping for a week on our bikes. After contemplating our navels for some time we settled on a trip to Maldon, a seaside town some 40 or so miles from Dagenham.

The next step was to persuade our parents to let us go but we didn't really envisage any opposition as most of us had been camping overnight with the boy scouts so were quite competent in pitching tents, cooking over a camping stove etc. I think we used to call it the art of woodcraft then.

Convincing them that we were competent to cycle the long journey on our own was another matter but in those days our parents were used to us going out at daybreak on our cycles and not returning until dusk so we were hopeful that they wouldn't need too much persuading.

Also there was not the amount of traffic on the road then and certainly no two lane dual carriageways to negotiate. It was commonplace then in the summer months to see families of cyclists heading off to the country or seaside resorts. It cost nothing and people could pitch their tents almost anywhere for free

Farmers generally welcomed cyclists and some of them had their own little cottage industries selling fresh milk, eggs and bread to the tourists.

Different times.

My parents also knew that I had a particular skill in the fact that I was a very competent map reader. I also had and still generally have the ability to remember every place I have ever been to by road and to retrace my steps without the need of a map.

Later in life whilst on shore leave in the navy, I never had a fear of travelling anywhere on my own in foreign countries.

I have never used a '*Sat Nav*' in my life and the only time I tried was using a companion's and the thing sent us the wrong way twice. Probably down to my own incompetence but if it was a choice between using one to save my life or rely on my own sense of direction, the latter would win hands down.

Please don't misunderstand me, they are a marvellous invention and have helped millions of people in all spheres of life but I clearly have a mind block towards them.

However I digress.

Our parents had been persuaded so we set about loading our bikes for our new adventure into the unknown. Panniers were fitted on our cycles and the tent and all the ancillaries we required were distributed evenly amongst the four bicycles. I said tent as in singular. This was our first mistake. We should have taken tents as in plural.

We had spent the odd night all together in a tent before whilst in the boy scouts but we were to find out for varying reasons that whilst we had one four man tent it would have been more beneficial to have had two tents for a week's camp.

The day we set off was beautiful and sunny and the journey was uneventful. We found a place to pitch our tent in Heybridge Basin a suburb of Maldon. Even to four young lads on the brink of becoming teenagers we admired the idyllic scenery around us.

We were all looking forward to a week of exploring the local area and not have to be home by nightfall as we did not have our parents to tell us what time to be in by. For most of us this would have been for the first time in our lives. Very grown up were we.

Being tired after the day's journey we settled for the night with the intention of an early start the following day.

The rain on the roof of the tent disturbed us throughout the night but our fatigue from the day's journey allowed us to get some sleep.

Daybreak came but the rain never went. For the next three days it didn't stop. Our groundsheet was soaked through and life wasn't very comfortable especially as we were all crammed together in this confined spaced. There seemed no point in making an effort to go out on our bikes as we would only have become saturated.

We managed in the brief moments there was a lull in the downpour to quickly fry some eggs to make sandwiches which was followed by cold drinks from bottles of squash.

Fortunately we had access to fresh water as the toilets were not too far away and every time any of us would have to go we would replenish our water bottles.

We had wet weather clothing but the rain was relentless. I can't even remember how we passed the time but as kids do various stories were probably recalled over and over.

Not yet being teenagers we didn't have the pleasure of being able to make up stories about our prowess with the opposite sex as girls then were just a pain and not worth discussing.

By the third day the rain hadn't stopped and in our minds we had a major dilemma. Despite being under cover, water seeped into every part of us and was starting to become irritating. The novelty of being away from home and having our independence for the first time in our young lives was starting to be less glamorous as we sat in our damp clothes.

Unusually for us we were starting to get terse with each other. We had always been good friends even though after we had split schools and I went off to County High, the relationship had remained firm.

We started to talk about going home but even that wasn't really an option as the thought of cycling 40 miles in this non- stop rain would be very unpleasant. Nevertheless it was possible and the thought of a warm comfortable bed and Mum's cooking at the end of the journey was an inviting prospect.

However we would be going back with our tails between our legs after bragging to all the other kids that if we felt like it we may even stay on for another week. We were adventurers and unlike them not tied to our mummy's apron strings we had told them. Foolish I know but we were only kids after all.

Whilst arguing over options our voices must have become raised as we heard a voice outside shouting 'hello is everything alright'?

When the flap was drawn back there was a man standing there in his early thirties I imagined but was probably wrong as gauging people's age when you are 12 years old wasn't an easy task.

He was covered in a heavy duty raincoat and appeared to be quite dry despite the rain pouring down it. He seemed genuinely concerned about the state of us all huddled together in this small internally soaked by now tent.

He motioned for all of us to put on our raincoats and boots and follow him. If for no other reason than a change of scenery we all immediately complied. Strange when I think back but here we were four young schoolboys following a full grown man into wherever he decided to take us.

Our parents if they could have seen us would have been livid.

There was no need though as he turned out to be one of the nicest and kindest men I've met in my whole life. I only wish I could go back and thank him for the way in which he came to our rescue. Sadly though despite wracking my brain I cannot even remember his name but as Vic is the nearest I can get to it for descriptive purposes I shall use it.

Vic led us to a really what we would now describe as a state of the art luxury tent. The canopy outside covered such a large area that he was able to cook without the rain falling anywhere near the camping stove.

Inside was enormous compared to most tents available at the time. He made us hot drinks whilst we explained our dilemma caused by the continuous rainfall. The weather was atrocious outside but as it was midsummer the temperature once inside an enclosed waterproof space was quite high. Compared to ours it was almost tropical.

After listening to our story he suggested that we all stayed in his tent for the night to dry out and he for proprieties sake would go into ours on his own.

This would enable us all to see if the weather would improve the following day and we could then make decisions on what to do. He himself had also had enough of the miserable weather.

As we were later to discover he was used to hardship so a night in a small tent was of little consequence to him.

We all whole heartedly agreed with his plan but to be quite honest I don't think any of us would have objected if he had stayed in his tent with us. There were no thoughts in our minds of any danger from this man.

People now because of the dreadful atrocities that have been uncovered over the years towards children would understandably be very concerned. We may only have been twelve but we would have known had we been in harm's way. To have been able to do anything about it may have been different but we would have known.

Regardless of our youth we had never been mollycoddled thus knew the way of the world. Despite having no concerns about him we ensured we were never individually alone with Vic both for his well-being as much as ours.

The following day after a dry night's sleep we awoke to more rain. It was now Wednesday and we were all feeling quite sorry for ourselves.

Vic popped his head into the tent to see how we were and recognised that we were down in the doldrums. He suggested that we get ourselves ready and for us all to go and find a café to get some hot food inside us. It was suggested that we could then make any decisions on a full stomach.

The thought was very enticing except for the fact that it would mean getting soaked again trying to find such an establishment. The trepidation must have been clear to see on our faces but quickly dissipated when he told us that he had already eaten in one a few days earlier and that it was only a few miles away in the car.

Wow he had a car!

Only two people in our street had a car and one of them was my brother and as he was rarely at home this would be a real treat.

After filling our stomachs we sat in the warm café and contemplated our next move. We were in no rush to leave and as we appeared to be the café's only customers due to the atrocious weather, the owner didn't seem too concerned about our reluctance to go.

Whilst it was still raining it wasn't by now torrential but the café was still much more inviting than a wet tent.

For young lads we were quite adult in our discussions about our plan but all agreed the whole trip had been a washout. No pun intended.

Vic explained that he was a Chief Petty Officer in the Royal Navy and was on four weeks extended leave. His plan had been to visit various friends he didn't get chance to see very often because of his job and as they lived in different parts of the country, mostly up north, he would take the opportunity to do it in a leisurely manner stopping off and camping at various locations on the way.

His unplanned long stop at Maldon had been forced upon him by the inclement weather. There weren't any motorways in those days and even in a car, trips could be frustratingly tedious.

There was the added problem that cars were not the reliable machines that we now take for granted and if possible long distances should be covered in short hops. They were apt to overheat, a common feature of most vehicles at the time.

As soon as the rain subsided and he could continue without the fear of heavy rain permeating his now ageing car, he told us he would be on his way.

He told us stories of the places he had visited in the world and as travel to foreign countries was unimaginable for us perhaps these tales remained in my young impressionable mind to such an extent that I knew then that at some time in the future I would try to get to sea.

We boys decided that we would give it at least one more day before returning home as that would give us credibility having lasted including our travelling time for six days. The brief respite from the weather we had by sleeping in Vic's tent had given us fresh momentum.

Vic offered us his tent again for the Wednesday night and we unanimously accepted. This was a kind and honourable man who put the welfare of four children before his own comfort.

Such a man would be difficult to find in these very different times. After a good night's sleep in Vic's tent we awoke refreshed the next day and even the sun decided to remind us of its existence.

After helping Vic dismantle his brilliant tent he bade us goodbye. We wished him God's Speed, a common farewell in those times.

As the sun was now shining warmly we resolved to have at least one day by the beach. Our tent was drying out nicely and our spirits were uplifted to the extent that we eventually stayed to the Saturday our original intended departure day.

Our return would be triumphant!

The last few days had made the trip worthwhile and being at an age when memories were short and the bad times quickly eradicated from our minds we had great pleasure in describing our wondrous exploits to as many of our other friends as would listen.

Not wishing to gloat we assured them that the following year we would allow as many of them that wanted to accompany us would be able to do so. Surprisingly we did the same in the next year's school summer holidays.

We did however venture further afield the following year to a place called Herne Bay on the Kent coast a distance of approximately 80 miles from home but the novelty of camping had started to wear off.

I remember the night before setting off, my eldest brother Fred took me to see the new 'box office' film at the time 'Some Like it Hot' starring Tony Curtis, Jack Lemon and the sex goddess Marilyn Monroe.

My parents had gone for a week to a holiday park at Clacton with my sister-in-law and their new grandson. Fred had to work so was unable to go and was left with the task of making sure I got away safely with my friends the following day.

I remember very little about the trip except that Cliff Richard was number one in the pop charts with Living Doll and we knew all of the words and sang it monotonously all of the time.

I think we went cockle harvesting whilst there but that was about it.

We had become teenagers and whilst still good friends the excitement was no longer there. Our bodies and minds were constantly changing and girls no longer seemed the pain that we thought they were the previous summer.

It was about this age that I got myself a Saturday job in one of the local army surplus stores. The store was owned by a man who along with his brother opened another venue in East London.

These stores were quite common throughout the country and entrepreneurs as we would now call them would buy surplus equipment from the government which was no longer required since the war had now been over for at least 14 years.

Conscription was also being phased out so there was even more armed forces stock available. Hence they were known as surplus stores.

They were generally given the name as Army and Navy stores to show patriotism or possibly just to make them sound less austere. Even this long after hostilities had ceased many items were still scarce and we were basically bankrupt after re-paying huge amounts of debt to the USA which had been loaned from them to enable us to conduct the war.

God only knows why they were not called the Army, Navy and '*Air Force*' stores as there was surplus from each of them.

Perhaps the person who gave them the name didn't like flying?

The owner was a brusque man and I initially didn't know how to relate to him. His manager at the store was called Mr Lamb and he always referred to him as Lamb not '*Mister*' Lamb, whether in front of customers or staff.

I always felt it was insulting and patronising to him to be called just Lamb as he ran the store on his own for most of the time.

The owner wasn't an unpleasant man, in fact completely the opposite and could be very kind but it was a part of his character I despised. He always referred to all of the staff by their first name so why not him?

There may have been history between them that we didn't know about but highly unlikely as Mr Lamb was a very pleasant unassuming man. He was probably only in his fifties but he was very old fashioned in his ways and attire.

If he tried to rebuke any of us it sounded more like he was apologising.

There was also a short dumpy woman named Aggie I think who appeared to be Mr Lamb's right hand woman mainly to assist him if any women entered looking for female apparel of which there was ever increasing amounts being stocked.

More and more women workers were realising that they could buy essentials at knockdown prices

The best way to describe Aggie would be to think of Miriam Margolyes without the ankle socks. There were times when Aggie tried to scold me but it didn't work. I had learned how to let my bottom lip drop and she would melt with shame at the thought of upsetting me.

The same could not be said for the girl who started working there full time and whilst helping me unravel parachute silk in the store room upstairs managed to position herself face to face with me as we came to the final fold. In one quick movement she slapped her lips coarsely against mine.

It was hard for me to tell but she was somewhere between fifteen to eighteen years of age and I was only thirteen for God's sake. By todays moral standards it was paedophilia on her part.

Nevertheless we tried it again just to see if I liked it. Which I did and visits to the store room became quite frequent. I did in her defence look older than my age

I enjoyed working there and it paid for my 'ciggies' and clothes as I had obviously now started smoking. It wasn't only all old surplus stock being sold.

There were days I would go into the store with an old pair of jeans on and come out with a pair of brand new 'Wranglers' which were now being introduced into the country from America. Cool Dude I was.

About a dozen shops away there was what was becoming known as a coffee bar where teenagers started to congregate and listen to their own pop music on juke boxes.

Many had been decorated to a modern standard with the latest coffee machines installed to cater for the youngsters who had more money in their pockets than their parents ever had before them.

The *'Wonder Bar'* hadn't though. It was a bog standard café with the owner pouring you an instant coffee with the obligatory cigarette hanging from his mouth.

No matter though as I was to discover there the magic sounds of The Everly Brothers singing Kathy's Clown on the juke box.

Genuine coffee bars were however springing up all over the country and they were generally warm comfortable places for youngsters to meet up with friends every evening if they so wished for just the price of a drink. Youth clubs were steadily declining in numbers as they were not the cool place to be.

There were of course some like 'The two I's' in Soho where the up and coming rock musicians of the day congregated and has now become a legendary establishment.

They kept the kids off the streets and continued to do so for several years for just the price of a coffee which wasn't in itself expensive then. These days an overdraft facility would be required to spend all evening in modern coffee houses.

After the first couple of years I lost interest in academic achievement but enjoyed the sporting life County High had to offer. I loved football and played in most of the school teams. I also played cricket but didn't enjoy it then very much as I was mildly bullied at times by other pupils into believing I wasn't very good.

I didn't understand it at the time and thus thought I wasn't any good and didn't realise until later in life that I must have been a reasonable player because no matter which team I played in, the teachers always made me opening batsman.

In any team in any class of cricket the opening batsman is always generally considered to be one of the best. Alternatively maybe the teachers were just warped and enjoyed seeing hard cricket balls being hurled down at me from the very first ball bowled. Pay-back for my lack of academic enthusiasm.

The bullying was probably because of jealousy by the less competent cricketers. It all however stopped when I later joined the school boxing team. I trained very hard after school and eventually became schoolboy champion in 1960.

I had to fight twice on finals night and it left a bitter sweet taste in my mouth. I had a lot of respect for my trainer until finals night when he told me after my second bout, (I was the only boxer who had to fight twice that night), that I got the verdict because it was a very close match the second one I had fought and the judges only gave it to me because I had fought twice on the same night.

I lost interest and all respect for him that evening. He should have just kept his mouth shut, if for no other reason than to avoid blunting my confidence.

The boy I had beaten in the second bout also said I would have beaten him even if I hadn't fought once already that night. A true gentleman. I became friends with him and some years later he moved into the flat above us in Dagenham. This was how boxers were with each other.

I have good memories of two of my older boxing team mates at County High, both of whom were a couple of years older. One was Josh Jones and the other Dave Munden who later achieved fame as the drummer in Brian Poole and the Tremeloes.

I later went on to the North East London boxing finals at Eton Manor but by now had lost interest and couldn't make the weight at the venue. I have always found though that when one door closes, another opens.

The night of the boxing final at Dagenham was also the night of the 4th form Christmas party at County High. Although exhausted, I managed to get home, get changed and get to the party. It was well worth the effort as it turned out to be one of the most memorable and pleasant times I had at school.

Word unbeknownst to me had got back to the party that County High had a schoolboy boxing champion. As I walked in, the music stopped and all of my year mates started to cheer.

A lovely moment.

It was even announced in assembly the following morning albeit grudgingly, by the headmaster, that the school had a Dagenham Boxing Champion.

Perhaps I am being uncharitable as I never got on with him but the delights of the previous night's party and the new found popularity with the girls more than made up for any misgivings I may have had.

I have since tried very hard to find a record of that night of the boxing finals without success. I think they were held at Halbutt Street but several schools had amalgamated and no records can be found, even if they were kept.

It was a different era to the all recording times we live in now. No matter though, I know it happened. I bathed in my new found fame for several months in the New Year but I now had my heart set on going to sea and travel the world. It was one of the only ways for working class youngsters to do so then.

GOING TO SEA

As previously said, back in the 60's you left school at fifteen years of age, except if you went to Grammar school, which then meant you had to stay until you were 16. Provided the school agreed though, it was possible to leave early if a job or career was available, as the legal leaving age was actually 15. Not like the rigid jobs worth times we live in now.

This was agreed to and I left with the intention of returning to take 'O' levels towards the end of the school term. I firstly worked at the British Market Research Bureau until it became possible for me to join the *Asiatic Steam Navigation Company (A.S.N.C)* in June of 1962. This was a quick way in those times to get into the Merchant Navy and avoided going to sea school at Gravesend for a year.

Times were very different in the early 1960's and I recall whilst still at school going with my mum for an interview to become a post boy at the British Market Research Bureau, Berger House, Berkeley Square, London W1.

Yes I know, unbelievable but my mum had to go with me as 15 year olds weren't considered responsible enough to make up their own minds. In those days you didn't become a man until the age of 21 was reached.

Indeed if you wanted to get married, it wasn't possible without the agreed consent of your parents. The alternative was to elope to Gretna Green. Even if I had wanted to, which I didn't, it would have been much too cold for me up in the wilds of Scotland.

I was interviewed by a kindly gentleman called Mr.Logie. He was a typical for the times city gent with the requisite bowler hat and umbrella.

He informed me that the weekly wage was £5.00, to be paid in cash at the end of each week. A princely sum to me as I had up until then had to rely on pocket money, and the Saturday job income from the Army and Navy stores. However it was a stepping stone to my future life and the amazing adventures I was to encounter.

Times were changing though and we were to see an evolution or revolution imminently arriving, depending upon your perspective at the time.

I've heard it said frequently that if you remember the sixties you weren't really there. What a load of old tosh peddled by people who were off their heads on grass or whatever substance floated their boat.

We didn't need that rubbish there were too many exciting times ahead. The next three years were the most exhilarating of my life. The staidness of listening to our parents' type of music, dressing like them as they had with their parents before them was to be swept away by the Beatles and the other Liverpool groups who were to follow them.

Elvis had been a revelation but the 'Fab Four' changed music forever. We had never seen such prolific writers.

I have clear and fond memories of all of the people I worked with in the short time I was at BMRB and I can only assume the reason that I can remember them all so clearly is because it was the transition from schoolboy to adulthood.

Jan was the boss of the post room and initially I thought she had taken an immediate disliking to me as another boy started on the same day and she appeared to be much warmer to him than me. Indeed she had remarked on her preference to another member of staff.

His name was Michael and I recall he was very well spoken, a stark contrast to me the youth with the unashamed cockney accent whose early playgrounds had been the East End of London bombsites.

Michael was a pleasant young man though and despite us coming from very different backgrounds we rubbed along very well together sharing the workload evenly.

After Jan's initial wariness of this brash young cockney she gradually warmed to me and over the short time I knew her we got on very well.

Jan had assigned me to a young man called Chris Speller to be shown the ropes as to how the mailing system worked.

Chris and I hit it off immediately and became good buddies. He I believe came from Shepherds Bush in West London. Sometimes in life you meet people who you immediately click with and he was one such person.

To ensure that staff arrived punctually there was a large lined book on a table at the entrance to Berger House and everybody had to sign in. It was part of Chris' duties to draw a line in red ink at 9am to show that anybody who signed the book below the red line would have been late. This would allow the company to take remedial action against persistent latecomers.

Throughout my life I have had a problem with timekeeping and I was no different then. Chris was well aware of it and went above and beyond the call of duty by delaying the drawing of the dreaded red line whenever possible.

He was ably assisted in this task at times by 'Mrs Mac' who worked in the binding room but occasionally was in charge of the tea trolley and thus could hover just inside the entrance to watch out for any managers who might decide to come down from upstairs to check that Chris was doing his job and drawing the line at 9 o'clock .

Chris would often stand outside looking for me to see if I was on my way and beckon me to hurry up so that I could sign in before he used his red pen.

To my shame there were many times when Chris had to stick his head above the parapet for me but in fairness to myself there were a lot of other people who benefitted from my poor time keeping as those who were also late managed to get signed in legally well after 9am.

Ralph from the print room who a year or two later I bumped into at Southwark Crown Court where he was acting as a juror, wasn't averse to taking advantage and would always give Chris a grateful wink.

I have 'Mrs.Mac's' daughter Val to thank for recalling his name despite over half a century has elapsed since then. I had struggled for years to do so.

We were never ever grassed up and I have always wondered whether Chris continued the ruse after my departure from the company because he hadn't done it before I joined.

'Mrs Mac' was very philosophical about it all and treated both Chris and I lovingly like naughty boys despite her complicity in the whole affair.

She was lovely as was her daughter Valerie McAuliffe who was 'a stunner' and also assisted at times in the binding room alongside a blond girl whose name escapes me.

Val's main office I recall was in the basement of a converted large house in 47 Upper Grosvenor Street near the old American Embassy in Grosvenor Square.

It was Chris' job to take documents to Val on a regular basis but on occasions Michael or I had the task and I have vivid memories of going down to the basement in the old fashioned concertina type gated metal lift.

Val I understand later went on to work for many years for the Ambulance Service as a passenger co-ordinator.

I think both Val and her mum came from Battersea and I have vague memories of sometimes walking to Victoria Station with them to catch our respective trains.

I will always be grateful to them and others for taking this naïve young boy under their wing in such a transitional period in my life. I am what I am today because of their example.

Despite the short time I was there I kept in touch with Chris when I left to join the Merchant Marine and attempted to send him a postcard from wherever I was in the world. I daresay had we then had the internet we would still be in touch today.

Despite extensive efforts and having the power of the net at my disposal, I have been unsuccessful in tracking him down.

He was very important to me as he was such a likeable human being and unbeknownst to me, when Ritchie a mate from Dagenham had come up to meet me for lunch, Chris had managed to illicitly have a word with him to find out what he thought I would like as a leaving present. Ritchie duly obliged and was spot on with his recommendation.

The reason for my departure was that the company had given notice that they were moving out of Central London to Ealing and although a generous offer was made to the staff, it was just too far for me to travel. I couldn't get to Berkeley Square on time let alone add another 30-45 minutes to my journey.

Chris would have still been waiting at 10am to be able draw the red line in the book.

Bless him he would have done it though.

The people there were so kind and generous but it was time to move on.

I had only been employed for a matter of months and when the time came to leave the last thing I expected was a leaving present.

Chris presented me from the staff an L.P. by the legendary guitarist Duane Eddy.

Still to this day I 'well up' when I think of this kind gesture.

It was called 'ESPECIALLY for YOU'

There was a card inside the sleeve of the record signed by the staff. Their faces have remained visually in my memory for six decades. Unfortunately the card has been lost after many house moves.

I STILL HAVE THE RECORD though!

BMRB were a good company to work for and were what we would now call employee friendly. They even subsidised our meals in the restaurant adjacent to Berger House which Chris and I frequently took advantage of.

They were substantially generous subsidies of the kind I have never encountered since. The real prices in the restaurant would have been out of reach for us.

This was after all Berkeley Square one of the most prestigious landmarks in the country.

I vaguely recall on the other side of the square the main Rolls Royce showroom dominated the thoroughfare but my mind may be playing tricks on me.

The subsidy would have been very expensive for the company but it probably enabled them to maintain staff levels in those times of low unemployment. In the ensuing years I remember looking with pride at the credits on 'TOP of the POPS' showing that the charts were compiled by BMRB.

I constantly bored friends bragging I had worked for them. This was after all the top music programme on TV.

All good things must end though and later in the same year along with the rest of humanity, I was to experience one of the most frightening events of my life.

The first ship I joined was the Motor Vessel Royal *Avalon*. A pleasure boat which sailed six days of the week from Tower Pier to Margate in Kent, stopping off at South end- on- Sea to pick up more excursion passengers. We tied up at the end of the world famous Southend pier which in those days and still has I believe, a miniature railway which ran from the pier entrance to almost the end of the pier. Sadly the Margate pier no longer exists.

When tied up at Margate we would take on extra provisions like crates of beer were it necessary. This occurred mainly at the weekends when excessive amounts of alcohol had been consumed. All '*on watch*' crew had to help get them by hand from the pier. It was very hard work especially for a 16 year old boy.

We would then take day trippers from Margate on approximately a one hour journey in a circle around the estuary. Seems pathetic now but in those days it was considered a real day out treat.

Some of the crew occasionally went ashore in Margate to get an hour away from the ship and I clearly remember one season that '*If I had a talking picture of you*' by Joe Brown and the '*Bruvvers*' was the hit song.

We spent most of this break in a coffee bar hearing it being played over and over on the juke box. God only knows why we didn't have a walk round the town instead. Probably because we enjoyed just watching the girls jive around in the small amount of floor space available to them.

The ship was full at weekends and for a 16 year old red bloodied heterosexual male it was paradise. The swinging 60's were taking off and I thoroughly enjoyed myself.

A bit like being in a boy band today, ship's crew were spoilt for choice when it came to the opposite sex. There were times throughout the summer when each night after disembarkation at Tower Pier, we had to send shipmates ahead to see if there was more than one girl waiting to meet us from those we had met on previous day's trips.

We had a good system going and whilst there were some lucky escapes, to the best of my knowledge none of us were compromised.

All the nice girls love a sailor was never truer than in those wonderful times. I made some good friends in the crew but unfortunately there were no mobile phones or internet so once you left a ship and joined another, you usually lost touch forever. This continued to be the case with poor communications remaining right up until the 1990's. Whenever I have spoken about this to my grandchildren they look at me as if I am from another planet.

THE *AVALON* 'TICKLES'

It is not my intention to brag or boast about that which is to follow, merely to put my view on the real world. People will always find a way to make money on the side and the summer pleasure boats were no exception.

Like all good parents should, mine tried to shelter me from the actuality of the real hard world that was to come for working class lads like me from the slums that were the East End of London after the War.

The *Avalon* was my first real eye opener into the world of '*tickles*' (fiddles) whilst cruising up and down the River Thames. Most of the crew all had their own '*tickles*'. On my first season on board in 1962 I was shown the ropes by some hometown mates who had served on previous seasons.

Ship's Provisions were taken on board, usually on a Friday as the ship didn't generally sail on that day to enable it to be prepared for the busy weekends that lay ahead. As I recall, only a skeleton crew were kept on board to allow the ship's company a day off before what was to be a hectic weekend with hopefully a full complement of passengers.

On the occasional Fridays I did have to work even my innocent eyes noticed that not too much attention appeared to be paid to stocktaking. Goods it appeared to me were loaded randomly from various victual suppliers and nobody seemed to have any interest in keeping track of what was being loaded

Perhaps this was because the Port of London Authority (P.L.A.) who I believe owned Tower Pier would only allow the *Avalon* to berth alongside for a limited amount of time therefore speed in loading was of an essence to avoid financial penalties. The fees charged to the *Asiatic Steam Navigation Company* who owned the *Avalon* were probably high even for those times.

The intention was to load as quickly as possible and get out to anchor I would assume. The *Asiatic Steam Navigation Company's* offices were in close proximity to Tower Pier so whether there were storage or refrigeration facilities attached to the buildings I don't recall but nevertheless as loading was completed expeditiously, it may well have been the case.

Logistically it would have been difficult to ensure that every supplier to the ship could arrive in such a small window frame of time on Fridays as there were occasionally several other ships needing replenishment, so perhaps they were pre-stored.

The thing I do remember is that there was a small car park in front of the *A.S.N.C.* office and the following season after purchasing my first car at the tender age of 17, which was almost unheard of in those days, I was allowed to park it there from Friday evening upon return to the ship, until my next day off on the following Thursday evening.

It would be unthinkable now with prime parking in London at a premium. Nobody in *A.S.N.C.* seemed to be bothered, probably because staff travelled into work by the Underground, Tower Hill Station being only a stone's throw away.

I would sometimes leave it there for weeks on end and never ever found a mark on it. There were no gates or CCTV cameras in those heady days and the blight of vandalism had not quite yet reared its ugly head.

I say my first car but it was in fact a blue Ford 5cwt 100E van. It was my pride and joy. I must say in all honesty that I never had a full driving licence at the time but small things like that never mattered when you were 17.

It certainly didn't stop my shipmates from riding with me and in fact *Nick* one of the Chefs who only lived a stone's throw away from my parent's house in Dagenham, used to accompany me home on most

Thursdays and sometimes of another evening if we fancied a night in our own beds.

Nick had a full driving licence so if we were stopped by the police the most that could happen was a fine for no 'L' plates. We never were stopped though.

Whilst we had to leave Dagenham very early the next morning to get back to Tower Hill there were hardly any vehicles on the road so the luxury of sleeping in a comfortable bed was well worth the inconvenience. It beat sleeping on the hard steel beds on the *Avalon*.

There was also the added bonus of being in a Chef's good books. Please don't ever think the most important person on a ship is the Captain. It's not.

It's a chef.

I ate very well that first season but to be fair all of the ship's crew did. To give them credit the company did not skimp on food.

I bumped into *Nick* several years later after popping into a café for a coffee in East Ham to find that he was the owner. The same could be said about '*Dodgy Doug*' one of the tea barmen on the ship. He had also opened a café but in Redbridge.

Why '*Dodgy Doug*?' I hear you ask. He wouldn't serve any crew member tea from his tea bar, not because he was tight and didn't want to give any members of the crew freebie cups of tea but because it was debatable as to what went into his tea beside the leaves.

He would always direct crew away from his bar and down to the galley if they fancied a cuppa.

I had it on good authority from his 'bar boy' that methylated spirit is a good tea strengthener. *Doug* would for example be expected to get perhaps 1000 cups out of a carton of tea but by the use of an additional substance he would get perhaps 1200 out of it. So for each carton it was 1000 times the price of a cup of tea for the company plus 200 times the price of a cup of tea for him. You never hear alcoholics complaining about 'meths' do you?

THE 'CHICKEN CARRIES'

Owning the van on the *Avalon* was a bonus in other ways as well. A few of the other higher ratings had licences and would sometimes ask if they could '*borrow*' it to pop home to see their families on the occasional evening. I didn't mind because their '*borrowing*' was my 'hiring'.

It supplemented my wages when the van wasn't in use and my rates per mile were significantly less than car hire companies so there was never any haggling.

The car was fully insured for any driver as dad had stipulated at the time when he stood as guarantor for the loan to purchase the car that this had to be the case.

The van was also handy for '*chicken carries*'. Chicken was roasted on an almost industrial scale and it was difficult to calculate how many pieces were required each day as it depended on how many people were on board that wished to eat it. The 'Pantry men' whose job it was furnish the stewards with the meals required for the saloons always seemed by accident or intent to have lots of chicken breasts, legs or thighs left over on a Thursday evening. Mainly breasts though!

As the ship didn't sail on Fridays and there was a limited amount of refrigeration facilities available on board, rather than throw the cooked chicken away, the crew, provided they didn't have too far to travel home, would be allowed to have it.

You could be forgiven for thinking how could they possibly take plastic bags of cooked sometimes even hot chicken on the Underground in the summer for any amount of time without the smell permeating around the carriages, especially if they were packed with commuters.

It wouldn't be long before other passengers were trying to move away from the offender as quickly as possible.

Many of the crew would therefore resist the temptation as there were no such things as supermarket type plastic bags in those days. We did however have old fashioned hessian type sacks from which most of the provisions to the ship had been carried in. Things such as potatoes, meat and other perishable goods were transported in these sacks.

There was no shrink wrapped containerised pallets then and most stores had been hand loaded onto the ship so there was a surplus of these sacks for use in our 'chicken carries.'

Strangely enough they held in odours and were much stronger than any of the flimsy things shops have to charge you for these days. If you didn't live too far from the ship they became an extra supplement to the family meal and in my first season I took full advantage of this perk.

We talk about austerity now as if it's a new phenomenon but it's not. In the early 1960's we were still suffering from being a bankrupt country because of the cost of the Second World War.

Fortunately within a few years austerity did end but in the late 50's and early 60's there were many a family who appreciated a nice bit of professionally cooked chicken for their dinner. My mum certainly enjoyed it.

The following season was therefore better as I had the van to take home as much chicken as I wanted without London Transport having to fumigate their carriages.

In any workplace environment there would always be conflict between employees but on the *Avalon* it was kept to a bare minimum. Everybody understood that one broken cog could cause problems within the chain of command and it was in nobody's interest to whinge or complain. Whatever your task was on the ship it was incumbent on you to do it to the best of your ability.

On my first season aboard, as a newbie I had to do mostly menial tasks such as scrubbing the decks on my hands and knees as there were no industrial cleaners on the ship.

I had to load heavy sacks of potatoes into peeling machines and once peeled distribute them to the galleys for the cooks to roast, transport large urns of milk up and down the galley corridors and any other dogsbody task which needed doing.

It was hard manual work but despite this less than glamorous life style I was actually at sea and wanted to see the world. I had got on with these chores without complaining and unbeknownst to me it hadn't gone un-noticed.

I had heard via the ship's gossips that a vacancy had arisen as a 'bar boy' in one of the bars. You didn't apply for vacant jobs as would have been normal shore side. Jobs were offered generally on the say so of the rating of whom you would be working for and as I had only passed the time of day in the mess with this particular barman rating, I didn't really give it much thought.

To my surprise, *Jamie* the barman in question approached me and informed me that he had been given permission by a Senior Officer to ask me if I wanted the job. I jumped at the chance.

I found out later that I had been recommended to him because I had gone about my work diligently and without complaint. There were other boy ratings more experienced than me, so I was pretty 'chuffed'.

ALCOHOL GALORE

Jamie was a pleasure to work with and he set about showing me the ropes. Fortunately one of my new found boy rating friends, *Gary Baxter* was already working in another of the bars so I had a rough idea what my duties would involve.

I call it a bar but it wasn't much larger than an average size council house bathroom. Wooden crates which held 24 x 1 pint bottles of beer would be stacked roof high at one end alongside cartons of various spirits.

Now this was how the system worked:

Passengers would come aboard in their hordes especially at weekends and make their way around the ship finding the various facilities available to them spread around the various decks. All of the bars remained closed until the ship left Tower Pier and made its way downstream after negotiating Tower Bridge.

In those times generally you could only be served an alcoholic drink between the hours of 10.30am until 2.30pm and from 5.30.pm until 10.30.pm. There were minor variations to these hours dependent upon which part of the country you were in.

One of the main reasons parties of mainly men in those days came aboard, was because of the liberal licensing laws on board. As a whole the bars were open from the time of our departure from Tower Pier at nine in the morning until returning the same evening.

As I remember they also closed whilst tied up at Southend and Margate. The actual bars on board were all pretty uniform so that in the event of sickness for example, a barman could transition from one to another and know exactly where everything was. Loss of alcohol selling time was frowned upon as the company only had the short summer period to make its money.

The bars all had a standard bar top with a flap which lifted at one end to allow access for the barman and bar boy. There wasn't room for anybody else. The floor was raised, whether by design or not I have no idea but it was impossible for passengers to see over the bar. This allowed for a multitude of sins.

Our jobs as bar boys were to sit with a giant funnel in our hand in the small area immediately under the locked bar flap.

The purpose of this was as follows: When the bars opened there was a general stampede by the passengers to be served first, so not too much attention was paid to the barman's trickery. *Jamie* would open each bottle by means of an opener attached just under the actual bar out of sight of the passenger and by sleight of hand would angle the bottle downwards so that he could pour about one eighth of the bottle into a large enamel jug situated below the attached bottle opener.

As he brought the bottle up he would adeptly shake it so that the beer would froth up and over the top of the neck of the bottle causing a large head in the glass thus the passenger had no idea that they weren't receiving the whole amount of the bottle for which they had paid.

Sometimes the passenger would ask for the bottle tops to be left on the bottle but they had no chance. *Jamie* along with every other barman on the ship had stock answers.

We had no 'off licence' they were told, so beer had to be served in a glass unless they wanted a crate of 24 pints but even then they had to be served to them with the bottle tops removed.

The reason being was that once *Jamie* had filled his jug with the elicit slop beer he had dropped into it he would pass the jug to me and replace it with an empty one. My job was to then fill up all the empty bottles with the slops from the full jug and put them into an empty crate. Hence the reason I had a giant funnel.

Crates were never served to punters until an hour or so after leaving the pier. The reasons given to the passengers were varied. They were told it was because either:

1. The crates had to be brought up from the holds so passengers would have to pre-order them.
2. Ships regulations stated that we had to be a mile downstream before it was safe for the crew to go into the holds.
3. Because of the vibration the propellers caused when initially started, it would shake the crates in the ship's holds so violently that they needed to be left for a while to settle.
4. Any other load of old bollocks the barmen could make up.

The real reason was that the barman needed sufficient time to fill his jugs with slops to enable the bar boys to fill up the empty bottles to make up full crates.

Any crates that left any of the bars were filled with at least some slops. It was considered sacrilege to give punters crates that weren't partially filled with slops.

It also provided the 'lounge boys' a chance to find the punters who had earlier ordered the crates and deliver the crates to them, for a small fee of course.

By this method of re-cycling, for every crate of beer consisting of 24 bottles the barman sold he made three bottles for himself.

As the day went on and the punters became more inebriated the higher the ratio of slops became, so that by the end of a busy day *Jamie* was making an extra four to five bottles per crate for himself. The barmen looked after their 'boys' very nicely thank you.

To be fair to the barmen I must give credit where it's due. The spirit measures given were always accurate. Very noble I hear you say. Well it would be had they not already been watered down as well.

Nothing left those bars without being watered down. Not even the water!

It wouldn't surprise me if the crisp and nut packets had been opened, some removed and then re-sealed. No Trading Standards or Weights and Measures on these boats.

Shortly after I started working with *Jamie* he was offered promotion to an Executive Officer position. I had hoped he wouldn't take it, as he was a lovely man and a pleasure to work with. Very calm by nature and I never heard him ever raise his voice to anybody.

Despite being under pressure, especially at weekends, he always gave off an air of peacefulness. Nothing ever seemed to faze him. You have to be born like that, as it was a gift that most of us would have died for.

In view of the fact that he was earning a small fortune and had done so for several seasons I did not at first understand why he decided to accept the promotion but as he told me, there comes a time when you have to say that you have had a good run and know when it's time to move on.

Greed is an inherent feature in many human beings and the art of not allowing this character fault to dominate must be adhered to whenever possible.

It was something that I have carried with me throughout my life. Never get greedy. I have seen several men fall by the wayside because of it. Two of them actually going to prison by taking unnecessary risks.

When *Jamie* received his officers' uniform he looked very smart with the gold stripes on his arm and he became the butt of several jokes for a short time but being a very tolerant man he took it in his stride and never took umbrage.

***TEDDY* THE BARMAN**

My new barman was a waiter called *Teddy Driscoll* who was a completely different character to *Jamie*. My first impression was not favourable and I found him a bit brash. I felt that the promotion to barman had gone to his head a bit. It was a sought after job on the ship and initially I felt a bit of humility would not have gone amiss.

As I recall but can't be sure, the reigning barman generally had a say as to who his successor was to be and to this end I understood that *Jamie* would have had his reasons for recommending *Teddy*.

Probably because *Teddy's* was the largest cash offer to *Jamie* for the recommendation. I am probably doing *Jamie* a disservice but it was greased palms that made the ship tick over so smoothly.

I didn't initially take to *Teddy* and with hindsight I think it was just a territorial instinct. He appeared to want to change things too quickly and a way of working which had been established over many seasons hadn't broken, so therefore it didn't need mending.

That evening I explained my feelings to *Gary* my forward bar boy mate about *Teddy's* attitude and then thought no more of it.

Ships were tightknit communities and if you farted in your sleep on Monday night, the whole ship knew about it by Tuesday morning. To give an example of this, one particular evening all of us boy ratings had gone ashore for a few beers and upon return to the ship one of the 'on watch' ratings signalled us to very quietly follow him to one of the cabins.

Now as far as I can remember there were approximately sixteen bunks per cabin but possibly more. They were very basic with none of the luxuries of modern ships. He ushered us in and it was plain to see that the curtains were drawn around one particular bunk and generally speaking if you returned from ashore and saw this you would try to be considerate and not disturb whoever was in the bunk sleeping, however in this bunk hanging out the end of the bed there were clearly four feet visible.

Now and again though not a common occurrence, if a crew member pulled a young lady on the days pleasure cruise and couldn't contain his ardour he would smuggle her into one of the empty cabins for a few hours fun.

Most of us never bothered with this as it was too risky. It was okay if you were sure that you could rely on the ships launch man to ferry the young lady back to the pier later in the evening but if anything went wrong there would be hell to pay.

Gary always the joker thought this would be an opportunity to have some fun. As the couple were obviously completely unaware of us, *Gary* decided he would join them in the bunk.

He quickly pulled back the curtain and to our astonishment two startled men's faces were a sight to behold. They had apparently drunk too much and fallen asleep. In those days homosexuality was a criminal offence and for gays it was very difficult to find private places to enjoy sex with each other.

You will probably recall that I said earlier everybody was out to make a few extra shillings on the *Avalon*. It transpired that these two gay men had been offered the chance of a bit of privacy in one of the ships empty cabins, for a fee naturally.

What they didn't know was that the crew member who had made them the offer had taken them to the 'games' room. Now this was a cabin used for another fiddle by certain members of the crew.

The thing was that as the day went on, some passengers would become more and more inebriated and would want somewhere to take the young lady they were with or had met on board, for some passionate 'nooky'.

The crew, always ready to oblige, would take them down to the 'games room' to allow them the privacy they craved. Now I hear you say what could be more romantic than helping the course of true love to flourish?

Well, sort of.

The cost of this privacy was measured in several pounds per hour of privacy dependent on the amount of time required. Being the *Avalon* the scam didn't stop there. There was no such thing as privacy. The members of the crew involved in the fiddle would already have lined up passengers who would like to see a bit of porn on the ship.

It must be remembered that pornography as such was an offence, so not readily available to the average man in the street. There was no shortage of takers. Again, at a price.

It must be said that we were after all on the '*high seas' (the River Thames would you believe),* so these sort of things were allowed. Well at least that's what the punters were told. Nobody believed this bullshit but if it helped the men, some of whom who would have been married or had girlfriends to have relief from their guilt, then the crew would have been providing a community service.

'How were the crew going to show this pornography? I hear you ask'

Perhaps pornography was not the right word but voyeurism certainly was. This is where the term 'games room' came into play.

It was the bog standard sixteen bunk steel hulled cabin with just one of the beds made up to accommodate the 'would be' lovers. As on most ships the interior walls (bulkheads) were made up and held together by thousands of steel rivets.

In seasons past, one or more of the steel rivets had been removed and replaced by a replica made out of cardboard or wood.

The carefully chosen made up bed could be seen through the rivet hole once the replica had been removed and any noise made by the 'pervos' looking through them would be drowned out by the noise of the ships engines seeing as all of the cabins were below decks.

The couple would have been blissfully unaware of the sex show they were performing for the paying 'pervos' looking through the hole. Nothing was sacred on this ship and nothing has probably changed in holiday type establishments where people gather for fun and pleasure ever since those days.

However, I digress. *Gary's* barman *Ricky* was the most senior of the barmen and on 'turn to' (start of work) the next day, *Ricky* could be seen in conversation with *Teddy* about the best way to run the bar and that any deviation from the accepted method would be met with disapproval by all of the other bar managers.

Whilst *Ricky's* tone was conciliatory, *Teddy* was left in no doubt as to what was expected of him. I actually heard *Ricky* say to him in a hushed voice, that *Teddy* would be wise to follow the lead of his bar boy if he had any doubt about procedure as they had all been chosen for their work ethic and loyalty.

It had not been my intention to cause any problems for *Teddy* but the conversation I had with *Gary* about my feelings had resonated with him and *Ricky*.

Nobody, to use an apt metaphor wanted the boat to be rocked.

On the next day which was spent at anchor, the mood between *Teddy* and I could not be described as friendly. He clearly hadn't taken kindly to being chastised by *Ricky* but I did however try to help him as much as I could.

As the day progressed I was starting to feel rougher and rougher and felt I had contracted a cold or even flu. Although it was only in the summertime that the ship sailed, there were more cases of head colds or flu than could normally be expected at this time of year but nobody seemed to know why.

The following morning I felt dreadful and failed to 'turn to'. As was customary, it was *Teddy's* duty to inform an officer of the watch of my non-appearance and it would then be the officer's job to find out why.

On this particular day it just happened to be *Jamie.* He came to my cabin to check on me and could clearly see the outbreak of the flu. He indicated that I could go home for a couple of days to recuperate if I so wished.

I declined and told him that I would rather stay on board to be available if necessary to help *Teddy* in case he needed me. This wasn't strictly true.

Bar boy jobs were like gold dust and I wasn't about to give mine up because of a bout of flu. I was too busy earning a fortune. Had *Jamie* still been my barman I probably would have gone home if for no other reason than to sleep in my own bed. As *Teddy* was a new barman and we hadn't exactly hit it off, it would have been a chance for him to get rid of me had he so wished to do.

Jamie allocated him a temporary bar boy for the next couple of days which were sailing days but apparently it didn't go too well.

Both *Teddy* and bar boy were inexperienced and there was a lot *Teddy* needed to learn. Not so much about the actual bar keeping but more about the fiddling. He needed an experienced bar boy to help him and none of the other bar managers were about to loan him their boys. They knew their earnings were affected by their boy's competence and speed.

Jamie had taught me all he knew and now *Teddy* needed me to teach him. This is how it had always worked regardless of rank. I 'turned to' on the Sunday morning, the busiest day of the week and to his credit *Teddy* seemed pleased to see me. Fortunately the ship wasn't packed to capacity, so it allowed us time to start to work at sea together.

The only other day he had sailed with passengers on board had been the previous one which was a Saturday and he had an inexperienced bar boy trying to help him. Through no fault of the bar boy it had been a nightmare, as they to use *Teddy's* words, "had been pissing in the wind".

We quickly became organised and worked so hard that day that by *Teddy's* own admission felt that now he had at least a good inkling as to how the system worked.

Upon cashing up on the Sunday night he gave me a wad of notes as a thank you but tempered it by saying not to expect that much every weekend.

The barriers had been broken down and for the rest of the season we earned a lot of money as well as becoming good friends.

My end of season bonus went towards a deposit to buy a car on my seventeenth birthday.

On the final night of the season, my fellow boy ratings and I returned to the ship via the launch. *Teddy's* bar was on the right upon entry to the ship and I could see a shaft of light emanating through the shutters. There should have been nobody in the bar as it was quite late, so we all warily approached the bar and listened.

There was clearly movement inside so as if we were one, we all kicked and banged on the shutters in an effort to frighten any would be burglar. There was a scream of "shut the fuck up" from inside and *Teddy* opened the bar flap and motioned me to go inside.

The rest of the lads said their goodnights and went to their cabins. Once inside I could see that *Teddy* had all of his stock books on the bar and was scratching his head in bewilderment.

Whilst it wasn't following etiquette for a boy rating to question his boss, I asked him what he was doing this time of night in the bar. After the ship had docked all bars were supposed to be customs locked until 'turn to' the next day.

He explained that he had to submit his stocktaking figures the next day to officials of the *Asiatic Steam Navigation Company* and as it was his first season as the bar manager, he had little idea what was expected of him. I had always been pretty good with figures so offered to help.

He was already two parts to the wind but was a man who could hold his drink, or so I thought. By the time we finished we were both so drunk, neither of us could see how to get out of the bar, so to the best of my knowledge, spent the rest of what was left of the night on the floor. To be truthful though, I don't really remember.

I didn't see *Teddy* again until the next season and as he was still the bar manager, it was clear our book keeping had been good enough to satisfy Head Office.

OFF TO SEE THE WORLD

After a season on the *Avalon* with occasional days on its sister ship the *Artemis*, which took holiday makers to France I was determined to go 'Deep Sea' as it was called and with my new seaman's ticket in my hand set about finding a ship.

After several unsuccessful attempts finishing up going only as far as Liverpool, Southampton and Glasgow I was starting to become despondent. I had been on one of the ships with another Dagenham lad named Keith and whilst in Liverpool we visited the Cavern Club and saw the Beatles.

The Liverpool-Mersey sound was in its infancy at the time and we didn't realise the significance of that night ashore but as the world became aware, we saw the greatest group of all time performing live within touching distance of us.

There are many tales to be told about the first twelve months in the Merchant Navy. I had been employed on another ship as the galley boy and my duties were to keep the galley (*kitchen)* and all its utensils spotlessly clean.

I highlight spotlessly only because that's how it had to be. If an outbreak of food poisoning or worse were to occur whilst Deep Sea, the consequences could be grave. There were no Accident and Emergency Departments in the middle of the ocean.

There were weekly and sometimes daily inspections by the Captain or ships officers to ensure cleansing standards were always high.

Now this was only my first time working directly under a Chef and whilst I knew my duties this was the first time that I had been asked to do an errand by any member of the crew whilst I was on shore leave.

I was going on shore to have a stroll around Southampton and as the only boy rating on the ship, I went alone. Every town was a new adventure for me as I was relatively new out of school and had never travelled much outside of my own hometown.

The Chef handed me a note with a bottle of Gordon's gin written on it. He asked if I could get it for him in an off licence whilst ashore. Now I was only sixteen at the time and off licences weren't supposed to sell alcohol to anybody that young but I knew I could get away with it as I looked older than my sixteen years and had purchased alcohol before without being questioned.

I agreed to do so as it would have been churlish not to and the Chef, apart from the Captain was the most influential person on board. He was after all the man who looked after our stomachs.

Whilst on a trip Deep Sea, the ship could do without one of the navigation or engineering officers but not without a Chef. I had noticed that this particular Chef always smelt of drink so I wasn't surprised when he asked.

He enquired as to if I had enough money on me to pay for it, saying he couldn't leave the galley for a while to go to his cabin to get money as he was so busy and that he would give it to me upon my return.

I wasn't too happy about this part of the favour but nevertheless agreed. I spent the afternoon strolling around Southampton, purchased the gin and returned to the ship and took it to the Chef's cabin only to find he was quite drunk.

He said thanks but made no attempt to pay me. I showed him the receipt and he said he would have to get it from the Purser's office the next day as he didn't have it in his cabin. As I had very little money left I was pretty pissed off but thought what the hell?

That evening I was sitting in the mess when one of the ratings, a guy in his late teens or early twenties struck up a conversation with me as I was obviously a fellow

Londoner. He was about to go ashore and asked if I fancied going for a pint. I explained I had no money because I unintentionally and reluctantly loaned it to the Chef because of the errand I had to run for him.

After I told him of the episode he seemed to cut the conversation short and left the mess. The next day I 'turned to' and found a new Chef in the galley.

He seemed a very affable guy and introduced himself which surprised me as boy ratings were the lowest of the low and it wasn't customary for Head Chefs to formerly introduce themselves. He told me to report to the Chief Steward's office before starting my duties.

I knocked on the Chief's door with trepidation, wondering what I had done wrong. He ushered me into the office and offered me a seat. Now I was getting worried. Chiefs generally addressed anything they had to say to a boy rating through another man rating. It was just etiquette.

He handed me some money and asked if it was enough to cover the amount I had loaned the Chef. I explained it was too much but he said I was to keep it. He thanked me and apologised for the behaviour of the Chef. He dismissed me with a kindly smile.

Sometime later the same day I was approached by the rating I had spoken to the previous evening whose name

I now knew to be Steve. He went on to explain that after our conversation in the mess the previous evening, he had gone straight to the Chief Steward and told him of the episode with the Chef.

Being a conscientious Chief Steward he immediately summoned the Chef from his cabin and summarily dismissed him after he admitted that the version of events given by Steve was true. The Chief knew that this would be problematical for the ship and the shipping company as they would have to find a replacement Chef overnight.

The ship actually being in Southampton didn't make things any easier but they managed it nonetheless.

This inconvenience was preferable to having the company's name being besmirched for employing a drunkard of a Chef who borrowed money from a boy rating to indulge his habit.

It was strictly taboo to borrow money off a boy rating.

It had never been my intention to cause trouble for the Chef but unknown to me he had already upset several of the crew and was generally disliked.

The officers of the ship were completely unaware that had the ship eventually continued on its trip to New Zealand, a favoured destination for Seafarers I may add, several of the crew were going to leave before coming under Articles (maritime law), should this Chef remain employed.

Nobody apparently fancied being away for months with this particular man in charge of their food. The action became unnecessary as everybody for whatever reason I know not what, was paid off eventually in Southampton.

To his credit the Chef came to see me before leaving the ship and now being sober offered his apologies to me. I explained that I had no intention of causing problems for him but that an innocent conversation had caused his downfall.

I understood that the company offered to re-employ him provided he agreed to seek medical help for his addiction which he subsequently did. It had been a magnanimous gesture by the shipping company in view of the inconvenience he had caused.

After being 'paid off' in Southampton, myself and Steve returned to London vowing to find a Deep Sea ship together. We met up a couple of times for a beer and he told me of the various places he had been in the world which was fascinating for me as I still hadn't managed to leave the country.

Steve managed to get signed up for a trip on a small cargo ship heading for the West Indies and told me there was a vacancy for a boy rating if I fancied a trip to the Caribbean. I jumped at the chance, who wouldn't? The ship was also due back in the UK before Christmas which pleased us both.

I was little prepared for the exciting times ahead visiting Kingston Jamaica, Haiti, Santo Domingo, Nassau, Bermuda and Port Antonio. Steve and I spent as much time as we could ashore, hiring scooters to visit the exotic islands. Dream land for a 16 year old boy.

The ship's galley staff were mainly exuberant West Indian's who were a pleasure to be around. They were all looking forward to setting sail for the West Indies to be able to see their loved ones and as we were due to be there for a few weeks it would give them the opportunity to spend time with their families. We didn't however envisage what we were about to witness on our journey across the Atlantic Ocean.

THE CUBAN MISSILE CRISIS 1962

In the winter of 1962 the Soviet Union was attempting to base nuclear missiles on the island of Cuba in the Caribbean Sea. The USA did not want this to happen, so they adopted an embargo in the waters around Cuba. The new young American President, John F Kennedy was not going to allow the USSR to put missiles on Cuba, thus giving them the opportunity to attack the USA from an island so near to the States.

This is just a resume of what was happening and anybody who wants to know the full story can look in the history books.

Basically Kennedy told the USSR Premier Nikita Kruschev that he was not going to allow it and that war would follow if Kruschev did not turn his ships which were carrying the nuclear warheads around and head back to the Soviet Union. History has shown us that it was the closest we had come to World War three and nuclear annihilation.

I do not know what the feelings of the British people were at that time but subsequently have learned that the world stood still for a while and everybody was fearful that Armageddon was nigh.

At the time all of this was happening I was on my first trip Deep Sea and was approaching the West Indies. 57 years later I can still recall hearing a large boom which looked like it had emanated from an American warship which was approaching us on the starboard bow.

What happened next I cannot vouchsafe as being the truth as it was way above my pay grade, to use the modern terminology. These are the facts according to the ships lawyers (gossips).

We had inadvertently entered the seclusion area set up to intercept the Russian missile carriers and were thought by the American gun boats to be a hostile ship.

Apparently the commander of the war ship had indicated to our Captain by Morse code, lamps or flag signals that we were to identify ourselves, stating our nationality, destination and the cargo being carried. International flags sometimes were not flown on the yard arm in international waters.

Here is where it gets tricky. In those days in the early 60's, our merchant sea Captains were mostly ex Royal or Merchant Navy some of whom would have served in World War two and believed Britannia still ruled the waves. I understand that our skipper was unaware of the international crisis and blockade and was not going to be dictated to by anybody in International waters.

He apparently changed his mind when the warship signalled to comply immediately with their request, or a shot would be delivered this time across our bow. A large Union Flag (which only incidentally becomes a Union Jack when it is attached to the yard arm of a ship), was quickly spread across one of the ships holds to enable aircraft to identify us.

I must clarify here that most of what I have written except the warship being in view and a boom heard is hearsay and the reader could be forgiven for thinking surely the Captains would have liaised by phone or internet or radio etc.

It must be remembered however that this was 1962 and when you crossed the Atlantic Ocean in those days and left London on a relatively small cargo ship, for the crew there would be little or no communications until you were in spitting distance of land.

We had no way of knowing of the tension that had been building around the world that Nuclear War was imminent. I can remember being shadowed for a short period by a warship until it peeled away to continue its duties, so normal relations must have resumed on the respective bridges of both ships.

We had been blissfully unaware of the situation until then but I can clearly recall the feeling of fear running through the ship. We were thousands of miles away from our homes and on the brink of nuclear war with no communications possible with our loved ones. A letter home took two weeks to reach the UK and that's after we eventually reached land and had the chance to post it.

Many of the crew were married with children. The thought of never seeing them again must have been hell. I was young, single and immortal as everyone is at that age and just starting out on the adventure that is life. I was not scared, well at least the '*wacky backy*' which I was shortly to try said I wasn't.

We had now reached Haiti and within a short time the world came to its senses and world destruction was put on the back burner and I was able to see the beautiful islands of the Caribbean through the eyes of a young man who had never been abroad except to France where I hadn't even managed to get ashore.

To this day I have never smoked '*wacky backy*' again.

Unfortunately I had a few surprises in store for me when we finally returned to the Royal Docks in London on a winter's day in 1962. My girlfriend had dumped me by letter whilst I was away but in fairness to her she had posted it weeks previously but as I have already said, our mail was always so far behind us.

It seems incredible now with the advent of email-Facebook-Messenger-WhatsApp, etc. Upon returning home mum told me my gran Eliza had died (Grandad Tom having died some years earlier) and to my eternal shame I did not feel much about it at the time as I was suffering the loss of my first love. At sixteen the world and your feelings are completely different to anything experienced later in life. You are still a boy but think you are a man and exist in your own little world.

I wished I had asked the questions about her passing but by the time I did it was too late.

'WORKING BY'

After being at home for Christmas 1962 I started to look for another ship. I had lost touch with Steve and never saw him again.

I shortly thereafter received a telegram asking me to report to the shipping federation ASAP. There was a flurry of excitement in my street because rarely did anybody receive telegrams. They were usually reserved to notify people of bad news as they were the speediest way to make contact if you didn't have a telephone, which in 1963 we didn't.

In fact nobody in our street had a phone.

Telegrams were very expensive to send but to large shipping companies the crewing of their ships for imminent departures far outweighed the cost.

The telegram was a piece of paper with a teletext type font stuck on them. We rarely had typewritten letters then simply because only public bodies and large companies had typewriters.

The arrival of the Royal Mail boy (Post Office as it was then) on his cycle, started the net curtains twitching in the streets windows and before the boy had chance to get the telegram out of his leather pouch, our house was surrounded by the local kids wanting to know what was occurring so they could tell their mums.

Sadly for her Daisy wasn't at home when the boy arrived and missed her chance of 'celebrity' with the neighbours. I recalled some years previously at the Council Town Hall the Mayor had shook her hand and she was so thrilled she didn't wash it for days. Different times.

I am sure though that later in the day she couldn't wait to speak to her friend Rose who lived several doors away, to fill her in on every little detail.

I know it sounds silly now but in those drab days anything out of the ordinary was a major talking point in the council estates throughout the country. The 'swinging sixties' was only just manifesting itself in our towns and cities with the advent of new music, fashion and attitudes to authority.

The telegram boy as if reading from a script said for all the kids to hear:

"I have a telegram for Mr A.P.Cotter, can you tell me if that is you sir?"

The street urchins looked at us in awe as they had probably not heard anybody they knew except for teachers, called 'sir' before.

I confirmed I was he and the boy handed me the telegram which said roughly:

'Report to shipping federation offices tomorrow…*stop*...bring seamans'discharge book...*stop*...immunisation documents...*stop*...vessel sailing in 3 days...*stop*...advise by return. *Stop*...

I read it out loud for the kids' benefit.

The telegram boy asked if I wanted to reply and he must have noticed the look of concern on my face. To reply was charged for by the word or letter, I can't remember which but I do know it was very expensive.

He immediately advised me that the cost of any reply would be borne by the shipping company. With his help I replied in the affirmative and offered him the telegram back but he assured me it was mine to keep.

I knew that Daisy would be thrilled and would compensate for her not being there when he had arrived. She could proudly show it to everybody in the street. None of us knew anybody who had received a telegram before. The world was a completely different place almost 60 years ago.

Shortly after I set sail on my first and last cruise ship. The atmosphere was completely different to cargo ships and I didn't enjoy the trip at all.

The crew acted as if they were in a holiday camp, which in a way they were. I wasn't keen on any of my shipmates as they always seemed to be sucking up to the senior officers in an effort to gain promotion and spend time with the passengers.

That wasn't why I was at sea. I wanted to visit new countries and if it meant going ashore on my own that was fine by me. I didn't mind my own company and had no fear of discovering new places alone. We sailed through the Mediterranean on through the Suez Canal and onwards down the Eastern coast of Africa visiting Dar-es-Salaam, Beira, and Mombasa, then down to Durban.

I enjoyed the entertainment the ship offered. The crews' mess or 'pig and whistle' as it was called, provided light entertainment mostly by the 'drag queens' on board. Apart from this I found the trip quite boring which was unusual for me, probably because I didn't make any friends.

It was the only ship I didn't meet at least one comrade spirit to spend time with. Whilst ashore I would sometimes visit the Seaman's Mission and partake of the sports facilities they generally offered.

I played football for one of the seamen's missions against one of the local African teams but by then I was on 30 Woodbines a day so was absolute rubbish. By half time I had difficulty walking let alone kicking a football.

I did however enjoy the trip through the Suez Canal which was a unique experience but was overtaken in later years by steaming through the Panama Canal. Both are awesome pieces of engineering. To be able to sail from the Atlantic Ocean through the Panama Canal and into the Pacific Ocean was an experience I will never forget.

The trip on the cruise ship was relatively uneventful except for being hospitalised in Mombasa with a throat virus. Fortunately however I was only kept in overnight and able to re-join the ship the following day.

Upon returning to London I vowed I would not sail on a cruise ship again unless it was absolutely necessary.

I never did.

<u>SECOND SUMMER SEASON ON THE *AVALON*</u>

After the normal complete cleansing of the ship by all of the crew, I assumed my role as *Teddy's* 'bar boy bitch,' as he liked to call me. Many of the following days were spent in a haze.

Drink then and still now was never really my forte but as a 17 year old boy with free alcohol on tap it would have seemed churlish not to partake of it. *Teddy* was a hardened drinker, so it was only sociable of me to join him. We had a lot of fun that year until I was promoted.

Teddy couldn't understand at first why I was taking the promotion, just as I didn't when *Jamie* did the same for different reasons the previous season.

He nonetheless wished me well and cursed me jokingly that he now had to break in a new bar boy. We both knew the truth had really been the other way round.

I didn't see him again for several years, until we bumped into each other at the Royal Standard pub in Walthamstow but alas I was with friends and were about to move on elsewhere and thus never had chance to catch up.

Another shipmate I never saw again. Such a shame we never had mobile phones or the internet at that time.

After being back home in Dagenham for a couple of days laid up with 'flu, I returned to the *Avalon* one lovely summer evening. I was picked up by a police launch and ferried across to the ship from Tower Pier, a quite frequent occurrence because the *Avalon's* launch generally only operated when the launch operator was sober, which wasn't often.

We always made a contribution to the Police launch box for the Widows and Orphans police fund, so they always ferried us to the ship if they could but there were many nights for one reason or another, normally another, I slept on Tower pier's concrete floor until the first ship's launch arrived at 5am.

There were very few people on board that particular night as the *Avalon* hadn't sailed that day so many crew members had taken the opportunity to get home to spend a little time with their loved ones.

As the weather was so nice I went and sat up on the lifeboat deck which gave a beautiful view of the Tower of London or upstream toward Westminster and the later to be shipped to the USA, London Bridge.

After a while I saw a police launch approach with two or three men on board, one being *Tommy Czerski*. I liked *Tommy* as we got on very well, even though I was a boy rating and he must have been in his middle 20's.

I thought he had seen me from the launch and waited for him to join me with a beer on the lifeboat deck.

Some days later whilst standing by the exit hatch waiting with the rest of the crew to dis-embark when *Danny Scanlon* the Second Steward approached and told me to report to the Chief Stewards office as there were detectives from Scotland Yard who wanted to talk to me.

I was gobsmacked and the first reaction was of panic but I knew I had done nothing wrong and was still naive enough to believe I couldn't be in trouble if I just told the truth. I was after all only 17.

They asked me about my movements on the night I had returned to the ship after the bout of 'flu. They wanted to know who I had spoken to upon my return.

I told them exactly what I had seen; just *Tommy* and a couple of other men come onto the ship in the Police open top launch. I hadn't recognised the other men but that wasn't unusual as the crew changed frequently, almost on a weekly basis.

This is where it gets difficult as they asked if *Tommy* had been talking to the other men and I told them, not that I saw. I gilded the lily a little bit here and said in fact that he had his back to them and was waving up at me on the boat deck and signalling as to if I wanted a beer when he arrived on board. Strictly speaking as a boy rating I was still too young to purchase alcohol.

By now I had realised that something serious had gone on, but the police were saying very little. They said I could leave but may want to question me again at a later date. It seemed like they had been questioning me for hours but it was probably more like minutes.

I promptly left, went ashore and joined my shipmates in one of the pubs at Tower Hill, probably the Tiger, which was then a stone's throw from the pier.

Upon entry I noticed *Danny Scanlon* was sitting quite close to the door which was unusual as he normally would not drink ashore with the crew, especially boy ratings, as it could have been awkward drinking with us of an evening and then have to be the strict disciplinarian upon 'turn to' the next day.

He immediately, pulled me to one side and asked me what I had said to the detectives. Now I may still have been very naive but I wasn't stupid.

I told him what I had told them and added that I also explained to them that I had not been well on that evening after just returning from sick leave and after about five minutes or so felt so rough I went below to my cabin and turned in to try and shake off the head cold I still had.

It was obvious the police knew that *Tommy* had also returned to the ship that night as it was a police launch that had ferried him across as they had done for me earlier in the evening therefore I knew I wouldn't have been dropping him in it.

I asked *Danny* what was happening as I really didn't have a clue, probably like most the rest of the crew. All I knew was it was about *Tommy* who was *Danny's* mate. What did surprise me was the fact that I had addressed him as *Danny* and not 'Second' and he hadn't batted an eyelid.

Normally if a boy rating called him by his name whether on board or ashore, they would have been scrubbing the galley deck and sun lounges each morning at 'turn to' for a week. It was always 'Second', not *Danny*.

He informed me that the night in question, armed robbers had entered the Pursers office, bound and gagged him and emptied the safe and that it had been kept under wraps until the police had chance to question everybody who had been on board that night.

He said the police thought *Tommy* along with other members of the crew may have been involved but as such they had no evidence to corroborate this. He asked if I would go to court and give evidence on *Tommy's* behalf if it became necessary.

I assured him that of course I would but deep down was dreading it. Nothing became of it though and life on board returned to normal.

Like all things in life we seem to look back and remember mainly the good times. In the early 60's, life in the Merchant Navy still had a romantic image bearing in mind that there were few opportunities for working class kids to see the world for free but nothing is free in this life. It was hard work.

This was none more so than when I was on the Royal *Avalon*. We rose at 6am and rarely stopped work until 9 in the evening. Fortunately at 17 years of age I had plenty of energy and still managed to get ashore most evenings and have a beer in the Princess of Prussia in Prescott St, Aldgate.

After the episode in the pub with *Danny*, he appeared to mellow towards me. Not so many beer carries (hauling on the beer crates at Margate pier each day). Not so many 'dressing downs,' when I 'turned to' late.

Life seemed to get just that tiny bit easier each day, until in the middle of the night on one summer evening *Danny* and other Officers came shouting down the companionways to get our 'hands off cocks and on with socks'

We were all made to assemble on the boat deck and informed that all of the crew latrines (toilets) had been ripped off the walls in an effort to stop the *Avalon* from sailing the next day. Apparently this had been done by some of the crew from the *Artemis* our sister ship which for one night only had been at anchor just the other side of Tower Bridge.

They had thought it was hilarious to carry out this act of vandalism. God only knows why.

The reason for assembling us on the boat deck was to lower the lifeboats and then for all of us to go over and sort out the '*Artemis* boys'. I've got to say there was no appetite from myself or any of my shipmates to do this in the early hours of the morning.

All we wanted was to get back to our bunks. Perhaps our lack of enthusiasm was clear to see. Thankfully common sense prevailed and we never did launch the boats. Apart from anything else it took at least 8 of us to wind the boats down manually into the water. There were no hydraulic lifeboats on the *Avalon* if my memory serves me right.

Search me what any late night revellers crossing Tower Bridge would have thought seeing the ship's crew assembled on the boat deck in the early hours of the morning.

A week or so later I was told by *Danny* to go and see him the following day as he had some news for me. He was having breakfast in the Forward saloon when I approached him the next morning.

I had 'turned to' late and didn't think he knew. But he did! It is over half a century ago but I still remember his tirade of abuse just because I reminded him that he had told me to go to see him about news he had for me.

It went something like this.

'You ####### no good worthless piece of ####. How dare you interrupt my breakfast which I've had to wait for despite 'turning to' at the correct time and all because I've had to wait for you to be found, but could you be found? No! Because you hadn't even bothered to 'turn to' on time. Now get out of my sight you useless piece of ####### before I have you up on the bridge in front of the old man (Captain).'

I think it's fair to say I stayed out of his sight that day for as long as I possibly could.

That evening we were on the return trip backwards to Tower Bridge i.e. the stern end became the front of the ship to lessen the wash which the bow of the ship would make thus avoid tearing other vessels from their moorings.

It fascinated passengers and quite understandably so, because the ship would stop in a wide part of the Thames, Greenwich I think and do a 180 degree turn so the rest of the journey was completed stern first all of the way back to Tower Pier.

This had the added advantage of allowing the ship to be pointing downstream when we set off on the next day's trip. There would have been insufficient room to turn the ship every day at Tower Pier in any case.

I was just enjoying watching the brownish white wash and taking in the unique polluted Thames odour emanating from the screws when *Danny* approached me and told me to report to the pursers office to be made up to a 'Man Rating'. I had not long turned seventeen and to be given a rating at that age was to say the least unusual.

My salary just shot up and enabled me to soon buy my first new car. I will never forget the grin on *Danny's* face when he walked away. Did I get the rating for being willing to help *Tommy*, I'll never know.

What did change though was my relationship with him for the rest of the season. It was now for all my youth, on a man to man basis. He never knew it but he taught me a lot about life that summer.

Like many other of my shipmates, I never saw him again after that summer season.

ASSASSINATION

In November 1963 again the world stood still.

I was on a ship anchored out at West Mersea in Essex. It was a 'ghost' ship with only about 10 crew members on board. We were taking it the following day to the Isle of Dogs in East London to be scrapped.

That first night on board was very eerie as the ship had no power, thus no electrics. We dined on sandwiches and our only light was from a 'tilly lamp' (a paraffin pumped contraption). A transistor radio was our only form of entertainment or contact with the outside world.

That night it solemnly announced that President Kennedy had been assassinated.

The engines were fired up the next morning and we sailed the short distance up the Thames Estuary, all of us in shock. This young President had touched the hearts of a new generation.

On the ships that followed I travelled again to the Caribbean and then onto the Pacific Ocean via the Panama Canal and onwards down the West Coast of South America, stopping at Lima, Santiago, Valparaiso and various other ports in Chile and Peru.

The shipping industry was slowly diminishing due to air travel and containerisation but nonetheless I had managed to see a large part of the world.

My best mate on the Avalon was Jimmy Thoirs who came from Hackney in the East End of London. We lost touch after leaving the ship until a few years later I bumped into him at the Royal docks near the seamen's mission. By then he had married one of the girls we knew from the Princess of Prussia public house in Prescott Street, Aldgate.

After this chance meeting we went our separate ways with the intention of meeting up sometime but never did. I learned some time later that they had separated and finally divorced. I heard of this news with sadness via *Gary* the bar boy on the *Avalon.*

Gary was working on a building site with a crew of Irish navvies and seemed to be earning well as testified to by the top of the range luxury car he was now driving. In the short time I had known *Gary* whilst aboard the *Avalon* he always did seem to have his fingers in many pies. We reminisced for a while and I thanked him for helping me back on the *Avalon* when he had spoken to his barman *Ricky* on my behalf.

At the time it seemed insignificant but it changed my time on the *Avalon* for the better. He laughed it off and said perhaps one day I may be able to repay the favour.

We were just starting off in adulthood and who could know what life had in store for us?

The next 7 years were spent either at sea or 'working by' throughout the docks in the UK. 'Working by' was a system by which you were not actually at sea, but nevertheless in the Merchant Navy.

It meant you were not under articles as at sea and thus not accountable under maritime law. It was a means that allowed shipping companies to pay off crew when a ship returned to the UK and employed qualified seamen as 'working by' crew.

This suited me down to the ground as when my first child Julie was born in 1965, I had no urge to go to sea anymore. The subsequent birth of Caron my second daughter in 1969 saw me quit the Merchant Navy.

The UK shipping industry was in decline as were our docks and had been since the early 60's. Whilst the pay was good it was sporadic and permanent work was now required as I had a wife Lin and 2 young children.

The time spent in the Merchant Navy was hard work but I saw places I would probably otherwise never have seen.

MARRIAGE

I met my future wife Linda, an apprentice hairdresser in the dance hall at the back of the Church Elm public house in Dagenham. It was the swinging 60's. We saw each other on and off for a couple of years and eventually married in 1965.

Lin's mum and dad were Bette and George who had a thriving greengrocery stall at the side of the public house in Church Elm Lane. We never got on at the start but several years later they both changed their opinions of me and thankfully assisted us in bringing up the girls, as both of us parents had to work because money was tight.

Bette, George, Daisy and Sam performed their babysitting duties admirably.

Before Caron was born, Lin, Julie and I had lived with Lin's mum and dad, her gran and grandad and then my mum and dad, before buying a new residential caravan which was sited at Takeley, near Bishops Stortford.

I had recently started work on the building of the new Victoria tube line and was earning very good money which enabled us to buy the caravan and get some longed for privacy. I had to travel into Manor House Tube Station in North London every day but as train travel was free for me and I worked flexible hours, things weren't too bad.

Lin got a job in the local jam factory and could take Julie with her. This broke the monotony for her and brought in a few pounds as well. We had left our names on the council house list and after about nine months received a letter offering us a flat in Dagenham.

Whilst we were pleased and immediately said yes to the flat, it gave me a problem with regard to the caravan. I had paid at today's prices approximately £24,000 and had not yet finished paying for it.

After moving into the flat we set about finding a place for the caravan to be sited. Bette and George had a chalet at Leysdown on the Isle of Sheppey in Kent and they had heard of a new caravan site opening at Sheerness a few miles from Leysdown. We quickly managed to get the caravan sited there.

Many happy times were spent in the caravan or at the chalet at Leysdown in the following summers. Julie and Caron occasionally had their friends Karen and Maria stay and I always seemed to be able to fit jobs in around Leysdown. How we all managed to fit into Bette and George's tiny chalet I will never know.

By now Lin was a fully qualified hairdresser and used to supplement her wages by styling the 'drag queens wigs' at the various clubs at Leysdown.

George's health sadly was deteriorating from Emphysema and he passed away in 1976 at Leysdown, after a blood clot on his lung. He had been a heavy smoker at one time and it eventually caught up with him. The place was never the same again for any of us.

THE DEMON DRINK

I don't think my grandchildren understand why they have never seen me drunk so I will take a moment and try to explain as this may possibly be the reason. When I say drunk I mean paralytic drunk not merry drunk.

All I really remember was walking along the road early one morning after being thrown out of the local 'nick'. I had no coat and recall feeling very cold despite it being the middle of summer.

I managed to find our flat and managed to get Lin to let me in which she was reluctant to do especially after receiving a visit from the police in the early hours of the morning. They had been trying to establish my place of abode and through my drunken rants they had managed to elicit at least what I thought was my address.

They assured her that they would release me once I had sobered up enough to be let loose on the world. To be honest she probably told them to keep me as long as possible as she had to get up for work in the morning and didn't want a drunken lout waking her up.

Apparently I had been out on the aforementioned Friday boy's night out when they found me asleep on the greensward in front of our first floor flat. I had been incoherent at the time so they threw me into a cell for my own safety.

I managed to persuade Lin to let me sleep off the remainder of the hangover whilst she went to work.

Upon awakening and not yet fully sober I managed to get myself dressed but was concerned that my coat was nowhere to be found. I remembered having it after finishing work the day before but since then could not recall seeing it.

The first call was the 'nick'. The desk officer firstly asked if I had been charged and I told him I hadn't. As if I knew?

He assured me though that I had and appeared to get great pleasure in telling me so. Can't blame him though because like most drunks he would have known I would surely have made a real pest of myself. Retribution one might say but no that came sometime later at my court appearance.

I was fined heavily. I am sure they also charged me for the bed for the night.

Enquiries showed that I did not have a coat with me when arrested and as I was still unaware of what had happened I was hardly in a position to argue the point.

I was about to go back home when I realised that I would have been paid the afternoon before and therefore would probably have put my wages straight into my coat pocket. Back in the day most manual workers were paid weekly on the last day of the week and in cash.

Obviously I was now in real trouble. It was bad enough putting Lin through the previous night's charade but now when she came home that evening after work I would have to tell her I had no money to give her for food or rent for the week.

If I was still suffering from the effects of the previous night's drinking, I rapidly sobered up and tried to remember my movements from the previous evening but I'm afraid my mind was a complete blank.

I only vaguely remembered leaving work but where I went after that was a mystery. It then dawned on me that I had walked to the 'nick' because my car hadn't been outside the flat but my brain was so scrambled I paid little attention to this fact.

I was getting increasingly worried as to what had happened. I didn't recall ever blacking out before and had certainly never experienced anything like it from drinking alcohol.

I quickly found a telephone box and was about to phone my best mate Dee when I realised that I had no money on me. Fortunately I knew he had a home phone as his company had paid to have one installed so that he could be called out any time of the day or night. What his job was at the time now escapes me.

I chanced a reverse charge call via the operator and luckily his wife Christine accepted the charges. I explained my predicament to her and she told me that Dee had gone to our local hostelry the Church Elm Public house but she had no knowledge of the previous evening's events.

I headed for the pub in the hope that I would find him there but as I had no money I had a long walk. Upon arrival I found him and a few of my other drinking pals at the bar. As was customary one of them immediately ordered me a pint and I started to enlighten them with regards to my predicament.

Everybody listened intently with grins increasingly covering their faces. Nobody said a word and I was oblivious to their lack of empathy towards me until finally Dee told me of the nights events.

Les who was the *'Guvnor'* of the 'Elms' as we called it, by now had come round from one of the other bars to hear my story. Les had put a spread on for Lin and me when we married and he could best be described as a real *'diamond geezer'*

The Elms had a reputation in the area as being a rough house but when Les was in charge it would have been sacrilege to cause trouble as everybody knew Les was the boss and he was respected by all the local hard cases.

I once saw 'Ginger Ted' one of the aforementioned, grab two lads and literally bang their heads together and toss them out of the door because they were giving Les grief about short measures in their drinks. They were obviously not regulars or they would have been aware Les didn't do things like that.

'Ginger Ted' wasn't a man to be messed with as I knew him from my days on the *Avalon*. Anyway I digress. Dee told me I had been with him and some of our other friends the previous night but for some unknown reason I appeared to be drinking heavily and as I wasn't causing anybody any problems nobody seemed to be taking too much notice.

News to me but apparently I was very merry and was even making a spectacle of myself by trying to sing 'Bachelor Boy' which was a hit song for Cliff Richard at the time.

One of our mates 'Little Pat' would often get up on stage at another of our '*drinking holes*' and do the same but he could at least sing. I couldn't.

As the night had progressed I had become more and more intoxicated to the point where Les got Dee to take my car keys from my coat and give them both to him for safe keeping as it was a warm night and I wouldn't need the latter in any case.

At closing time I had appeared to sober up a bit and Dee and Barry, another mate, put me into one of their cars. Upon arrival at the flat as was usual I invited them in for a coffee but they declined as neither wanted to incur Lin's wrath considering the intoxicated state I was in.

Apparently I had no trouble in walking the 50 yards or so across the greensward in front of the flats to reach the stairs. I seemed to negotiate them without any problem so they waited a few minutes and left.

What happened after that is pure conjecture but it can only be assumed that in my drunken state I decided the warm soft grass of the greensward appealed as a comfortable bed for the night as I couldn't find my keys to get in without waking Lin. This is where the police officers apparently found me.

Les jokingly called me a few obscene names and then handed me my keys and coat with my wage packet unopened in it.

I had been a lucky boy plus the fact that it appeared I couldn't have paid for a drink all night as my wage packet was still intact.

Had I not been amongst friends the night could have been catastrophic but I learned from it and never consumed alcohol to excess again. In nearly half a century I never since have had a night's drinking and lost control.

A GANGSTER'S CHAT

On one particular Friday boys night out I was in the City Arms Pub on the Isle of Dogs when a couple of the drag queens one of whom knew me from the clubs at Leysdown, invited us to a party in a basement flat in Manor Park, East London.

Parties in those days were completely different to those of today. Although there was music it wasn't head banging, couldn't hear yourself speak music. It was continuous but still conversations could be had.

Both I and my mates *Patrick* and Georgie had been mingling with all the others at the party as people did in those times when I was approached by a young thick set dark haired swarthy man who engaged me in conversation.

I recall the other people I was talking to slowly one after another moving away from us and with hindsight later realised why. I was left talking to Ronnie Kray one of the notorious twins and whilst he said nothing which to many young men would have seemed anything but innocent, I recognised the signs of being chatted up by a gay man. His sexual orientation at the time was not generally known by the public at large.

As soon as the chance presented itself, *Patrick*, Georgie, 'Crystal' the drag queen and I quickly made our exit from the party to avoid any unpleasantness which may occur.

I had been on ships with many gays and knew as a passably attractive young man how to avoid advances from men but this was something more sinister.

Indeed I had some good gay mates and had always found that as soon as they knew you weren't '*trade*', (gay yourself), they never bothered you. Ronnie Kray was known to not take 'no' for an answer.

If my memory serves me right, practicing homosexuality was still an imprisonable offence then.

I had made a good friend on the *Avalon* called Brenda. His gay name was Brenda but I can't remember his actual name. He was a real 'queen', as homosexuals were then called and diced with danger by being camp outside of a ships environment.

He was the *Captain's tiger* (Captain's steward) and on one particular day on the *Avalon*, I and my mate Jimmy had noticed him being waylaid by a few drunken passengers, so we stepped in to stop things getting out of hand.

Within minutes despite the ship being full many of the crew were quickly in attendance and the drunks were soon dealt with but unfortunately like most drunks, they didn't know when to stop.

When the *Avalon* returned after its day trip it would sail under Tower Bridge which lifted its road bridge every morning and evening to allow us passage. We would tie up alongside Tower Pier, disembark the passengers and then pull away from the pier and anchor out 50 yards or so from it. The crew who needed or wanted to go ashore would then get P.L.A launches across to the pier.

<u>THE VIOLENCE AT THE TOWER</u>

On this particular day, the earlier drunks accompanied by more of their boys' day out friends decided that they didn't want to get off at the pier. The ship only had a limited time to disembark passengers and get to anchor, or they incurred large fines from the Port of London Authority.

This was explained to the alcohol infused mob in a very polite but determined way by the Second Steward, *Danny Scanlon.* The boyos were having none of it.

The mob of about 20 men were at the top of the stairs, (companionway*)* leading down from the Sundeck Lounge. *Danny* along with *Tommy Czerski* and half of the ship's crew behind them showed me something I have never seen the like of before or since.

Danny gave 'the mob' five seconds to come down and exit the ship, or they would be forcibly removed. This was greeted by hails of laughter and ridicule by the mob. Silly boys! Now *Danny* was regarded as a hard man but didn't look it. He was over six feet tall and wiry and nobody ever seemed to argue with him.

There were some Dagenham boys on there who were hard cases themselves frequently in and out of prison but they always treated *Danny* with respect. Until then I hadn't fully understood why.

Before the count of five was even started he savagely beat the first three ringleaders, until their blood was splattered all over the companionway. It was brutal and there was little resistance thereafter. The mob capitulated very quickly and left without *Danny's* mate *Tommy*, even throwing more than one punch.

As I recall the ship had to remain tied up to the pier until medical assistance arrived for the drunks. I am sure it was one pleasure cruise they never looked back on pleasurably.

The shipping company were none too pleased either.

The next day, several police officers with permission from the Captain came aboard to investigate the injured parties complains. Ships captains in those days were still quite powerful.

I don't know how true it was but I was reliably informed that the police officers after leaving the ship suitably refreshed decided no further action seemed appropriate against any of the crew.

After this little episode, Brenda became a good friend to me and my buddy Jimmy and there were no strings attached. Whilst we were only boy ratings, we weren't going to let any boozed up idiots take liberties with one of our shipmates because he was gay.

Brenda was a full rating and paid about four to five times our wages but would always bung us a few bob if we were skint and had pulled a nice young lady who we wanted to take for a drink.

The 60's were in full swing now and there were rock boat days featuring many of the Liverpool sound bands. They had little appeal for us as it diminished our chances with the girl day trippers as they now all seemed to want to go out with a musician, but I'm not complaining. It had been a marvellous summer.

THE ‘TEA LEAF’ YEARS’

My daughters were growing up quickly and it was a time when both Lin and I were working as hard as we could to get the girls as many things as they needed in their formative years. As any parent will know unless you are lucky enough to be wealthy it’s a struggle but worth every moment.

Like many others we tried to find ways to supplement our income. Times were hard but nothing like the times our parents had endured during the War Years and thereafter. I make no apologies for the things I got up to as I did it for my family and never hurt any individual person physically or financially.

As religion dictates we tried to install in them that it was wrong to steal but as in religion they could decide when they were older what is right and wrong. Our so called political role models were and still are ripping working class people off left right and centre.

To give a few examples, there was a government minister who tried to justify his excessive use of expenses which we all paid for by saying he had to use taxis to get to work in the House of Commons because of his unsocial work hours. He just didn’t get it that millions of people who worked unsocial hours had to get to work by public transport but he was in his own warped world different to everybody else.

He had made this statement on the BBC Question Time programme and was derided by the audience and later even by his own wife for talking like a '*pranny*'

Along with many others feathering their nests there was one in particular who had boasted of fiddling his expenses but this time on 'Have I Got News for You'. He had been claiming expenses for the upkeep of two houses until caught out by the Press.

The Press have many faults but if it hadn't been for them, those thieving MPs would still be milking the system.

What was this MP's punishment I hear you ask? Prison, de-selection, a night in the stocks?

No: a knighthood, followed by a ministerial post in the government. He can still be seen pontificating on various political programs and being fawned over by certain so called TV journalists.

They should get real and not give him the time of day. No proceedings were ever pursued against either of them.

The tragedy is that the public then re-elect them to parliament in what is an elitist corrupt system. For centuries we have boasted to the world of our 'Mother of Parliaments' but the recent Brexit fiasco has shown this fallacy up for what it is. Broken.

However so as not to show political bias, there was also the case of the opposition MP whose party's policy was that children should be State School educated. Where did she send her offspring? You've got it. To a private school.

Her excuse being, that all parents want to do the best for their kids. What about the rest of the kids who don't have rich parents?

Incredibly today there is still another shadow government minister using the same pathetic excuse. If they believe in their party's policies so much then they should adhere to them.

If they had any conscience they would give their almost £80,000 salary and their expenses to a homeless charity. They won't though because they are all too greedy.

Can anybody ever recall a 'financially poor' MP?

Many TV political interviewers whose job it is to question them have now become complicit with them being part of the establishment themselves.

What I am about to tell you is insignificant compared to this load of charlatans.

I only thieved from-multi nationals who ripped us off every day and are still doing so with the help of some of our greedy politicians who themselves are often millionaires. It makes me feel physically sick when I hear politicians say that they could earn much more outside in the real world than the amount they receive in salaries as MP's.

SIMPLE. Go and do it. Most of them are only feathering their nests for when they are eventually kicked out of power.

The pompousness we hear from MP's about there are no victimless crimes when they leave less fortunate people than themselves relying on food banks to feed their families.

My life as a '*Tea Leaf*' (thief) really started in earnest when I became a driver for a company named *Terry Parry* Haulage based in East London.

I had been sent to collect a load of home massaging machines which were then to be delivered to a company in Wembley. I was new and pretty naïve about professional driving at the time and so when it came to delivering them I counted off the required amount and had the delivery note signed.

I only had the one delivery to do but still had an amount of machines left on board. I had loaded them from the collection point myself and whilst doing so thought they had given me more machines than I should have actually had.

The machines in today's money were probably worth about £200 each and I had 20 still on the van. The only problem was I didn't know who would want to buy them. I quickly found a phone box and contacted my eldest brother Fred at his local club.

This place over the next few years was to become a regular drop off point for me with any ill- gotten gains I procured. One of Fred's drinking partners lived above an empty shop adjacent to the club so we stashed them in there until I could ensure there would be no comeback. Unfortunately for one particular driver who worked at the same company as me, having this storage facility available subsequently landed him in prison.

Fred and John, another elder brother, had been lorry drivers for several years and knew where to place stolen goods. After ensuring the machines had not been missed, they were duly found a new home and we all met in the club a few days later and shared out the proceeds.

In the following months I quickly learned about the '*fell off the back of the lorry game*'. The lack of security in those days of major companies beggared belief and even as I am writing almost 50 years later I am astonished at the amount of goods we were able to steal.

There was no need to be a bank robber or for that matter a robber of any other institution and chance going to prison for a very long time.

Just be a lorry driver and have a network of people who could place (*fence*) any type of goods. I would generally find at least one loader in most companies who would be prepared to put on '*extras*' for a price.

Everything which follows is not said to boast but merely to show how easy it was.

Whilst working for *Terry* we were contracted to collect goods from a large electrical distribution centre. As drivers our job was then to deliver them all over the UK.

Security was abysmal and most of *Terry*'s drivers had their own '*bent*' loader there. None of us let on to *Terry* but he had probably done it all himself. We just didn't want to implicate him at all.

Terry had a small fleet of trucks mostly Ford Thames Traders many of which were beat up wrecks. Some of them spent more time in the yard being repaired than doing actual deliveries.

Over a period of time all of the drivers came to know that if it became necessary they could drop off their extras at various locations known only to my brothers and myself. They did so in the knowledge that the goods would be safe until they could collect them later or simply leave them to be sold by us for a fee.

They were always treated fairly and thus nobody ever had a grievance with us. They named the price they wanted and if we couldn't sell it for that price they had the opportunity to collect their extras from our lock ups without being charged, even for the few days' storage.

At the start of the working week the drivers would descend upon the electrical depot to load up with goods for delivery throughout the country. We all, or at least those who had home phones, knew each other's numbers as back up should we break down with '*extras*' on board. The vehicles were so unreliable that it was necessary to have somebody available to help out whenever needed.

In the event of a breakdown and the necessity for a tow recovery back to the yard, so as to not implicate *Terry* we tried to avoid having any extras on board but it wasn't always possible.

If the police were to do a random raid (which happened quite often at haulage premises in those days) then *Terry* wouldn't have been compromised.

Whenever we had '*extras*' loaded onto the vehicles it had to be put on first so that the legitimate goods would hide it. This had its drawbacks though. It meant that all of the deliveries had to be done first before they could be got at.

We would sometimes be away from home for a few days and had to hope we could get back to unload the '*extras*' without breaking down.

If we were local it wasn't too much of a problem as one of the other drivers would rendezvous with the stricken lorry and transfer the '*extras*' before the tow truck was called out. If it happened a fair distance away it became a problem as happened to me on one particular occasion.

I was on a journey somewhere up North and before I had started my deliveries the engine malfunctioned near Leeds. I had to wait hours for *Terry*'s breakdown truck to reach me and tow me back to the yard.

It was the early hours of the morning when we arrived back at the depot. The legitimate load was obviously still on board which in itself wasn't a problem but there were also a load of '*extras*' wedged in front of it.

It would have been impossible to offload in the early hours, especially on my own, without causing suspicion to local residents or a passing policeman. Yes in those times they still patrolled on foot.

The following day upon arrival at the yard, one of my co-conspirators was there engaged in maintenance duties. He was waiting for his empty vehicle to come out of the workshop once extensive repairs had been completed. The plan he was told was that he, *Terry* and *Micky* the transport manager would then transfer my full load onto his empty vehicle and he could then do the deliveries whilst mine went into the workshop for repairs.

After explaining my predicament to him, we both knew we couldn't let that happen. Fortunately his vehicle wasn't expected to leave the workshop until the next day and the transfer wasn't going to take place until then, so we had a bit of time to come up with a plan.

We decided that later on that evening after making sure *Terry* and the other office staff had left, we would return in our cars, unload the goods on my lorry onto the floor, retrieve the extras and load it into our cars and then put the legitimate load back on my lorry.

All drivers had keys to the yard as vehicles left and returned at various times throughout the week. As was common in those days there was an old boy who acted as a night watchman but he was open to a '*bung*' so that didn't present any problem. CCTV in the late 60's was unheard of in transport yards.

That night we returned to the yard in our cars only to find that his repaired empty lorry had been pulled out of the workshop and my full one was now locked inside.

The night watchman was nowhere to be seen. Things didn't look right and there was nothing we could do so we quickly left the premises.

The following day we were called into the office by the transport manager. The offices were immediately to the left of the gates upon entry into the yard. Without further ado *Micky* the transport manager asked us why we had entered the yard late the previous evening in our respective cars and then left the premises shortly thereafter.

We obviously had no idea how he knew. He was generally a cheerful man and rarely showed anger but on this occasion we could see he was having difficulty controlling his emotions.

Terry was in his office adjacent to us with his door ajar which enabled him to hear what was being said. I found it strange that he wasn't taking part in the discussion but all was shortly to become clear.

Micky made it abundantly clear that we were only going to be given one opportunity to tell him the truth. His manner convinced us that the sensible thing to do was to comply.

I explained that my lorry as he knew had been towed back into the yard a couple of nights before after breaking down with its load still on board but that there were more goods on board than I had delivery notes for.

I told him that rather than implicate *Terry* I had asked *Dave*, the other driver, if he would come back to the yard that evening to help me unload the goods onto the floor, take off the extras put them into our cars and re-load the legitimate load.

Unfortunately we were unaware that *Dave*'s vehicle had been pulled out of the workshop and mine locked in there, which we assumed was for security reasons hence we left without the extras.

Micky appeared to relax after my tale and explained that he and *Terry* had sat in the office in darkness for the whole night to see who came into the yard.

Apparently a phone call had previously been made to *Terry* threatening to set fire to his vehicles, probably from a disgruntled driver or a rival transport operator who had a grudge against him.

This was the nature of the business which could be cut throat at times and as a result they both sat in the offices overnight when calls like this were made, in an attempt to catch the perpetrators should they attempt to carry out the threats. There would have been no need to call the police as they would have dealt with any necessary retribution.

Micky went straight out, locked the gates and came back in. He clearly didn't want anybody to see what was about to happen. This looked ominous for *Dave* and I which must have been clearly reflected in our faces.

He motioned to us to follow him to the workshops and to our relief along with the mechanics, started to help us unload the stolen goods into my car, minus a few bits for himself and the mechanics. Fair do's!

As we lived near each other *Terry* gave me a lift home in his sports car occasionally but the incident was never ever mentioned. If ever there was any comeback he could put his hand on the bible and deny any knowledge of it.

Terry and *Micky* were good mates and I am glad I didn't get on the wrong side of them as they weren't the sort of people you messed with.

Many other driving jobs followed throughout the 1970's. Both my brothers and myself had built up what some people may say was a dubious reputation for placing stolen items.

I rarely worked for a company for the wages alone, as driving jobs were generally poorly paid. Anybody with an ordinary driving licence could, if they were able, drive large vehicles. The criteria being, if you can't get a job doing anything else, drive a lorry.

Thankfully things were beginning to change and new licensing laws were gradually being brought in, necessitating proper instruction and testing to obtain heavy goods licences. This consequently for a time raised wages, as there were fewer and fewer heavy goods drivers immediately available to employers.

After leaving *Terry*'s employ I worked briefly for a hardware company delivering dustbins, garden forks, lawnmowers, shears and all other gardening implements. I was very silly because in hindsight I could have started my own B&Q warehouse as nothing of their like existed at the time.

Instead of 'stack them high, sell them cheap' my motto could have been 'nick them quick and sell them quicker'.

There was very little we couldn't get rid of. No thinking about it, there was nothing we couldn't get rid of. My parents' garage was like Aladdin's cave. Both Daisy and Sam had worked mostly in factories throughout their lives so had a large network of workmates who were always on the lookout for a bargain.

Think of any item that you would like to have and at some stage either my brothers or I would have been able to get hold of it. From a bar of soap to champagne, we could get it.

Around this period I was driving for a detergent company via an employment agency and on one particular day had stopped off at home for a cup of tea after finishing my deliveries.

There was a tendency for the cases containing washing up liquid to break open due to the pitching and rolling of the lorry once the majority of the load had been delivered.

Whilst waiting for the tea to be made I started to mop up the spilt liquid so it didn't stick to the floor. This enabled me to stack and secure any returns cases that had toppled over without getting liquid stuck to the soles of my shoes whilst unloading upon return to the depot.

I had the roller shutter of the vehicle partly open with only my body visible from the waist down. If I was ever thieving the one thing I would do would be to ensure the whole shutter was completely open as it looked less suspicious.

As I wasn't up to anything and was just doing a bit of housekeeping on the floor of the vehicle I didn't bother fully opening the shutter. Two men appeared at the back of the vehicle and asked what I was doing. They had their warrant cards held aloft so I thought it prudent to enlighten them.

Apparently they had for several minutes been routinely sitting in an unmarked police car watching my actions and as they could only see the bottom half of my body their suspicions were understandably aroused.

I fully opened the shutter so they could see the residue of the liquid still clearly visibly slurping around.

They seemed satisfied with my explanation but didn't look wholly convinced, so for some reason and I cannot explain why all these years later, I said to them "did you think I was stealing because if so you can come indoors and have a look around? In fact the kettle's on if you want a cup of tea".

What on earth was I thinking?

Thankfully they had seen me pull up and not take anything inside so fortunately they declined my offer. I say fortunately because had they done so they would have been hard pushed not trip over the cases of football boots in the hallway I had dropped off the previous day and were waiting to be picked up by one of my regular customers. Lucky eh!

I say lucky but in fairness to myself this '*Tea Leafing*' went on for about a decade and this was the nearest I had come to being caught. I wouldn't mind but even then it was only because I was being conscientious by cleaning up the floor. And they say honesty pays!

THE SMARTEST DRESSERS IN TOWN

By now along with one of my childhood friends Dee, I had been driving quite regularly for the aforementioned employment agency. These were days in which you were paid cash in hand for your labours, generally at the end of the week.

Times move on and the world rapidly changes as rightly it should. The alternative would still to be living in caves as hunter gatherers. The things we accepted just half a century ago today would be totally unacceptable.

Whilst broken down in Nottingham, I had occasion to stay overnight in a lorry drivers bed and breakfast

I call it a bed and breakfast in the loosest of terms as the stay consisted of sleeping in a metal single bed in what could be classed as a large barn. There were approximately 30 other beds and breakfast consisted of 2 slices of toast and a cup of what was described as tea.

It was in fact what we used to call '*gnats piss'*. A yellow coloured cup of water. The toilet facilities were situated in a Nissen type hut with a long urinal running along the length of one side of the hut and cubicles with half doors on the other.

Along the centre was a trough with about six taps all with cold water running from them perched on a continuous metal pipe with the idea being that the water would run continuously into it allowing the water to be scooped up into your cupped hands to wash your face.

The owners clearly had never considered installing hot water let alone showers or baths. Different times.

Long distance lorry drivers were treated with disdain compared to their continental counterparts. God only knows what any driver from mainland Europe would have made of the facilities afforded to British drivers if they had been unfortunate enough to have to journey to our shores.

Luckily for them it was before us joining the EU (then known as the European Economic Community), thus foreign drivers were few and far between. After Britain did join and more European trucks came, facilities slowly improved for our drivers as the Europeans weren't prepared to put up with our nineteenth century hostelries.

Truck drivers in mainland Europe were used to individual rooms, good food, good parking and most of the comforts of home.

Fortunately I only had to spend one night in this dump of a so called bed and breakfast as my vehicle had been repaired overnight. This place wasn't alone in its total unsuitability as I was to discover on another overnight stay in the middle of winter in Durham.

I had arrived just too late to deliver a load of furniture to a school and my disappointment was exacerbated by the fact that it started to snow quite heavily and the thought of spending the night in the lorry with no heater was not a pleasant prospect.

It was probably too late to find a bed and breakfast and as I had not expected to have to stay in Durham overnight I had not pre-booked a place to stay. I had plenty of blankets so I consoled myself to the thought of having to spend the night in the vehicle. A certain amount of heat could be attained from the engine cowling which was situated inside the cab but it was to say the least negligible

In order to be able to leave the diesel engine running all night to have a modicum of heat I sought out the nearest garage to fill up the tank.

I thought I had hit lucky when I struck up a conversation with the garage attendant whilst he was filling up the tank. He was a young man probably in his early twenties who I must admit I found to be a bit of a strange character.

I made the mistake of explaining my predicament to him with regards to having no accommodation for the night. He told me he knew where I could get a bed and that it was quite nearby.

Due to the fact that it was such short notice I expressed my concern that there may not be any rooms available. He said that he was due to shut the garage shortly and he would take me there and introduce me to the landlady and was sure she would be able to accommodate me.

I was uncertain about his eagerness to help me but thought perhaps I was just being too cynical. Geordies I often found were generous helpful people but this man didn't have the accent so I assumed wasn't a native of the area.

By now the snow was pretty heavy and I didn't fancy being cocooned inside the lorry all night. Despite my reservations I accepted his offer and in due course after putting his cycle in the back of the lorry we set off to find my bed for the night.

We quickly left the built up area and were shortly out onto country roads. As the weather was becoming increasingly hazardous I questioned him as to how much further there was to go and whilst I was in mid speech he pointed to a large old country house which in appearance was like something out of a Dickens novel about a quarter of a mile ahead. It was completely isolated.

An imposing lady probably in her mid-fifties answered the door and my new best friend whose name I now forget introduced me to her and explained my predicament. She affirmed that she did have a bed for the night and could offer dinner and breakfast the next morning both of which would be extra.

After agreeing the price we were ushered inside which was just as foreboding as the outside. She led me to the room in which I would be sleeping.

The room was large with about six uninviting single beds installed and the toilet facilities were communal and situated about 20 yards along the corridor. I recall making a mental note not to consume too many beverages that night as I didn't fancy having to get out of bed too many times in this cold inhospitable place in order to go to the loo.

I felt very uncomfortable but in view of the atrocious weather conditions outside there was little else to do but to try and make the best of it.

There was no warmth in the landlady and everything she said was matter of fact. I thanked my new best friend for his help and she informed me that dinner would be served in the dining room in an hour's time. After giving directions as to where the dining room was both she and he left.

Dinner was served and I was surprised to find my '*bestie*' sitting at the table. I started to think that my first impression about the weirdness of the situation was correct but was trying to be positive and thought perhaps the landlady had just offered him dinner as a thank you for getting her a booking for the night as she appeared to have no other guests in my bedroom on this particular evening.

In itself this would have not been particularly strange but apparently there were 4 other bedrooms all consisting of 6 single beds, none of which were occupied.

I quickly ate my meal which was not exactly filling, thanked my *'bestie'* again for his help and retired to my bed. It seemed that I was going to be the only guest in the establishment.

It was still very early in the evening but the house didn't appear to have a television lounge or come to that any other entertainment facilities.

There was nothing else to do but snuggle up in my bed with a book and try to get a good night's sleep if possible. At least there were plenty of blankets provided which was just as well as the whole house was like a freezer.

I had just made myself comfortable when my new *'bestie'* entered the room and started to open the bedside cabinet in the bed immediately opposite mine.

Now I really was starting to get concerned. Since meeting me in the petrol station and on the journey to the house he had made no mention of the fact that he was staying at the house also. Indeed there had been plenty of opportunity at the dinner table to tell me that he was sharing the same room as me but he chose not to.

His conversation whilst eating had been vague and uninteresting and although I had been grateful to him for his help in finding me a bed for the night the thought of sleeping in my cold cab was starting to become more attractive.

I was starting to find the whole situation bizarre and by now had no intention of engaging him in any form of conversation and resolved shortly to put my book down and try to get some sleep.

It had been a long day which was about to get even longer.

Before I had time to do so he approached me and started to prattle on about much he liked staying at the house as it was in the countryside and allowed him to be able to wander in the forest and mingle with the wildlife.

He said he had an air rifle that the landlady allowed him to keep in the house to enable him to go out and shoot the rats which plagued the house at times. He asked if I would like to see it. Before having chance to decline his offer he showed me a large knife he kept for use whilst out foraging.

It was all probably quite innocent but I had grave reservations about staying in the place any longer. I could see that the snow was even heavier than when I had arrived but I was feeling extremely uneasy and decided to go and sleep in my cab.

It wasn't rational I knew. I had sailed the oceans of the world through storms and cyclones but had never felt as vulnerable as that night.

It was still quite early in the evening but without another word being said he turned and went to his bed. Within minutes the sound of his loud snoring permeated the room.

I was comfortable in the bed and the thought of going out into the cold snow disturbed me more than the *'nutter'* in the bed opposite. Needless to say I didn't sleep a wink that night.

As soon as day broke I was out of my bed and away.

Sod the breakfast I had paid for!

The down side of casual work was that it involved phoning the agency each evening if you required work for the next day. Some days there was no work and some days we didn't want any depending on what type of jobs were on offer.

I was quite used to this way of working as our shipping industry was in decline thus providing fewer 'working by' days. Containerisation was having a major impact on our London docks. Deep water ports like Felixstowe were transitioning to this type of cargo as they could cater for the gigantic container vessels.

We always had in mind which jobs were likely to involve a '*tickle*'. I had started driving via the agency for *Grantham Textiles* and whilst it meant travelling from Dagenham it was quite regular work.

One of their drivers was off long term sick and the company didn't want to commit to employing a new full time driver until they knew how long he was likely to be off for.

I spent more and more time driving for the company and the manager appeared to be happy with my work ethic. He had used agency drivers for several years to cover for holidays and sickness but the standard of drivers provided had been unsatisfactory at times.

The company was located in an area which was known and controlled by the Basildon Development Corporation (B.D.C).

Basildon and the surrounding area had for some years been an overspill town for London. Council house building was progressing at a prolific rate. The only problem was that to qualify for one of these properties an applicant had to work within the Basildon Development Corporation area.

Lin, the girls and I were living in a nice maisonette in Dagenham at the time but the opportunity to move into a new house in the then up and coming new town was too good to miss. I applied to the B.D.C. on the grounds that I had been working on a regular basis in the area.

Shortly after, we were offered a house on the newly built estate at Laindon a suburb of Basildon. It was obviously quite an upheaval but we felt that long term it would be better for us all.

Most of our friends and family lived in the Dagenham or Romford area so it wasn't going to be easy but the opportunity to improve our living space and our quality of life outweighed the disadvantages.

After moving in and getting Julie settled in the local school we set about decorating the place. We had a car and whilst Lin didn't drive we were still able to get back to see family and friends on a regular basis.

Within a short period of time Lin struck up a friendship with one of our neighbours. Marion and her husband Dave had three young daughters who were similar in age to Julie and Caron. Marion originated from the West Country and Dave from Manchester.

We became friends and along with the girls started to spend time together.

I had been a good boy whilst working at *Grantham*'s and had not had one 'tickle' until a guy called *Ben Purcell* started work on the loading bay. We immediately hit it off sharing a similar sense of humour.

Part of my duties each Friday was to load the vehicle at about 5.30am and deliver the clothes and accessories to shops throughout the county. Until *Ben* started, it was *Brian* the manager who would help me load but his work load was increasing by the day and the company had reluctantly decided to employ somebody to assist him.

As he was responsible for the smooth running of the factory the early start each Friday was starting to take its toll on his health. Whilst he was a relatively young man it was clear he needed some help so the company albeit grudgingly employed another pair of hands.

There was already one driver off on long term sick leave and another winding down to retirement.

After a few weeks of showing *Ben* the ropes, *Brian* gave him the keys to the factory to enable him to open the factory on Friday mornings to help me load.

By now I had been offered a permanent job and after the required financial remuneration had been made to the employment agency by the company, I became an employee of *Grantham*'s. It suited me now to be employed on a full time basis. There is nothing new about zero hours' contracts as they have existed all of my working life in one format or another.

However I digress. One bitterly cold Friday morning I arrived at the factory in my newly acquired *Grantham* tailored suit, yes they gave us suits to make us look smart whilst delivering to the stores but no topcoats to stop us freezing.

Ben was just opening the shutters. My teeth were chattering with the effect of the cold winter morning. Within minutes he went into the factory and returned with a few nice topcoats and offered them to me to try on for size.

I thanked him but played coy as if I didn't understand what he meant but I did of course and the die was cast. I knew then that we were going to earn a lot of money.

Don't ask me how I knew when somebody was bent, I just knew.

At one particular National Freight company I worked at, I was told repeatedly by all the old hands that whilst there were opportunities for small 'tickles' with the day loaders, the night loaders were untouchable.

These were the men who under supervision loaded most of the vehicles overnight and then parked them in the relevant bays. We never had a chance to talk to them as they were always clocking off in the morning as we were about to start our day. I never spoke to any of them but tried to remember their faces just in case I should ever see them outside of work.

By pure chance this foresight paid off.

Whilst working at this company I hired a brand new top of the range Ford Granada Ghia to go on holiday to Blackpool with Lin and the girls. We as a society weren't yet using BMW's etc. as our first choice family luxury cars. European and Far East manufacturers didn't yet have a foothold in our car industry.

I had just filled the car with petrol ready for our trip when just by chance saw one of the night loaders going into the local betting shop. I am not a gambler but found this opportunity too good a chance to turn down. I parked the car right outside the betting shop in anticipation that I may be able to impress with it. There were no parking restrictions then so I was able to park almost immediately outside the door.

I went into the betting shop spotted my prey, filled in a betting slip and waited for the loader to approach the cashier. As soon as he did I got in the queue behind him. I quickly got into conversation about recognising him from work. After five or ten minutes of dialogue we left the betting shop together.

I offered him a lift in the Granada as I could see how impressed he was with it. He asked how I could afford such a car on the paltry wages we were paid. He had to do nights to bump up his earnings. The line had been cast and now had to be reeled in.

I told him about one of the day loaders with whom I had regular '*tickles*'. The night loader knew him and although it was a bit of a risk, I said he could do the same with me if he wanted to. The risk was worth it. From thereon '*extras*' could be found on my vehicle on a regular basis

I always paid the loaders regardless of the contents of the cartons whether it was expensive perfume or sink plugs. I knew from my day loader that the other drivers paid him a pittance for their '*extras*' so it was more in his interest to look after me first because I paid him so well. Some of the drivers would tell him that it had been worthless rubbish in the carton he had put on for them and thus gave him nothing.

I never did that. He was paid regardless of contents.

He also arranged for other loaders to put '*extras*' on my vehicle. He then paid them from the money I gave him, less his commission. I only ever dealt with him as was the case with the night loader.

They and I were on fabulous money.

This went on for months until I felt it was time to quit whilst I was ahead and there were other opportunities on the horizon. My mantra always was 'don't get greedy'. I had not forgotten what *Jamie* from the *Avalon* had told me.

After I left I heard that my day loader upped the rates for cartons he wanted from the drivers to compensate for what he lost by my departure. Up until the time he had started loading for me all the other bent loaders had been poorly paid by the drivers for the risks they had taken.

I believe he later became the bent loaders 'shop steward' and negotiated carton costs on their behalf. A cottage industry of '*extras*' had been born.

Talking of shop stewards I '*sold*' my loader to the firm's genuine shop steward. At a price of course.

At one stage whilst working there we had been on strike and one of the conditions management imposed whilst negotiations were taking place was that before there could be any return to work there would have to be an agreement that there would be 'LESS THIEVING' by staff.

In other words management accepted a level of stealing but not too much. The reason was that management had their noses in the trough as well. It's what made the world go round.

Back to the freezing cold winter morning at *Grantham*'s when *Ben* had offered me the topcoats. I had never actually been in the factory, as the drivers turned up in the morning and collected their vehicles which had already been loaded (except the Friday run), so I had no knowledge as to how stock was managed etc., and if articles were taken how long it would be before they were missed.

I quizzed *Ben* about it and he gently took my hand as if I were a small child and led me into his empire to show me the shambles it was. It would have taken a large computer which didn't even exist in those days to be able to make any sense of it. They clearly had no idea of the quantity of stock they were holding. It appeared that the machinists just made clothes and put them on the nearest rail.

Ben and I were now part of the rag trade.

Thereafter each Friday we helped ourselves to as much as we wanted, within reason. I know it doesn't seem possible now but it happened. There were no computers as I said and the attitude was just keep making the stuff and everything would sort itself out. Believe me I have to ask myself how companies could act so lackadaisically but they did.

As always there was a ready market for all the items and a network of '*sellers on*' was quickly established.

My two best friends Dee and Westy became the two best dressed men in town. Suits with collar and ties were commonplace apparel in those days so their wardrobes were varied and smart.

Dee sold clothes on at his place of work and Westy was the clothes king of the Holloway Road Pubs in North London. After his death, Westy's wife gave me a *Grantham* tie he had kept ever since those halcyon days.

I had also started collecting quality shirts and shoes from a new factory and it hadn't taken long to find a willing loader to assist me in my enterprise. Quite quickly orders for '*extras*' were being taken.

Christmas was rapidly approaching and there were plenty of buyers constantly demanding my wares.

On the Friday before Christmas I returned to the factory after completing my deliveries only to be confronted by the sight of two police cars parked in the yard. *Ben* was in the factory in deep conversation with *Brian* and uniformed and plain clothes police officers.

My heart sank as simultaneously they all turned and looked in my direction. I thought the game was up as *Ben* started to point at me as I was sitting in my lorry and definitely making no attempt to get out of it.

I decided to sit tight and try to look as nonchalant as I could by shuffling through my delivery notes. Two plain clothes police officers started to approach me and my first instinct was that *Ben* had been caught thieving and was going to implicate me as well. The arsehole, was my first thought.

My mind was racing as I tried in those in those few seconds to remember if I had any stolen goods at home but my brain just froze. I knew as soon as night followed day that the next step would be for them to search my house.

They introduced themselves to me. *Ben* was standing immediately behind them so they could not see the huge grin on his smug face. The bastard! To this day and I don't know why, as they started to speak I realised that we hadn't had a tickle that particular morning so provided there was nothing to incriminate me at my home, I would have been in the clear for anything missing that day, however my frazzled mind wasn't functioning properly.

He asked if I had filled up my lorry with diesel that morning from the tank in the yard before embarking on my journey. I have got to admit I found this a strange opening question about any clothes which might have been missing from the factory, however I tried desperately hard to think whether I had or not.

The look of anguish on my face appeared to make *Ben*'s grin grow larger and larger. He appeared to be enjoying my predicament too much for my liking. For some reason my mind cleared and I remembered I had filled up the night before, as I knew there was a tanker due with a delivery early on the Friday morning.

My thinking on the Thursday night had been that the tanker driver may be loading the company fuel tank whilst I was there Friday morning and it may have delayed me in getting away on time.

I then explained to the officers that I hadn't filled up that morning and gave the reason why. As quickly as they had approached, they thanked me and headed back into the factory with *Ben* in their wake, still with a huge grin on his face. I was shortly to find out the reason why.

Once the police had gone he told me that when I had left the factory that morning ,the fuel delivery driver had arrived shortly after and transferred fuel into our tank but unfortunately had not put the amount in he should have. **What a thieving bastard**!

It had been common practice for the fuel company's drivers to deliver early in the morning without anybody from *Grantham*'s being there to check the right amount had been put into the tank, probably because they were too tight to pay anybody the overtime to check it.

Quite accidentally the fuel tanker driver had been caught delivering his ill- gotten gains, being the fuel he had stolen from us, to a transport yard the police had under surveillance.

You just couldn't trust anybody. A lot of thieves about the police had subsequently told *Grantham*'s management.

Who would have known eh?

This theft had probably been going on for years as none of us drivers ever had to make a note of how much we put into our vehicle tanks. If the person responsible for ensuring we always had enough diesel in the yard tank couldn't be bothered to keep check, why should we?

The company were lucky that we were all honest and didn't steal any for ourselves especially those who owned diesel cars. To the best of my knowledge none of the drivers ever did. We were too honest for our own good I think you will agree.

Ben took great delight in seeing the look of panic on my face when I was being questioned by the police. He knew it wasn't about our '*tickles*' as the police had already told him they were just trying to establish the amount of fuel which had been stolen and until they could ask me if I had filled up that morning, they couldn't be sure.

He knew I hadn't filled up and could have told them so but decided to have some fun at my expense. The warped git!

No mind though, the amount of '*tickle*' money he was about to receive from me was substantially reduced that week.

Now who's warped?

To celebrate our 'great escape' I went to the local TV rental shop and ordered a Colour TV to be delivered and installed before Christmas Eve. Colour TV's had only just come onto the market and were quite expensive. We didn't know anybody who had a Colour TV within our family or circle of friends but the quiet Christmas we had planned never materialised.

Television then would close down at midnight but we made sure we never stopped watching until the National Anthem played and the final black dot appeared on the screen.

Normal service was resumed as soon as possible upon return to work after the Christmas Festivities. People never tire of buying new clothes if they were cheap enough and I now had Lin, Julie, Caron and a new Colour TV to support.

On a warm spring day I returned to the factory and noticed an unfamiliar man sitting on a chair next to the loading bay. He was wearing a Chef's uniform and had obviously taken the opportunity to get out of the kitchen and have a smoke.

As I approached the loading bay he appeared to be staring at me to such an extent that it was almost intimidating. His face appeared to lose its colour despite being a warm sunny day and I was starting to be concerned about his manner. It was as if he was fixated

Brian the factory manager came out to greet me and it was clear that he also noticed the Chef's vacant stare. This Chef was standing in for the regular guy and I had not seen him before, yet his face seemed familiar. *Brian*

asked him if he was feeling alright to which he replied that he had been until he had seen me.

He asked if I had been in the Merchant Navy and if so, had I served on a small cargo ship which sailed on a regular service to French, Portuguese, Spanish and Italian ports around the Mediterranean? A lovely route in summertime but could be scary in the winter.

The 'penny dropped' and I recognised him as one of my shipmates from the aforementioned ship. The Chef had obviously recognised me before I had him.

The last time I had seen him which was several years before, was in a barbers shop in the infamous Cable Street in the East End of London and although I didn't know him very well we had struck up a conversation about life on board.

The topic of conversation which I didn't really recall that much of was the impending sale of the ship to a Greek Shipping Line. The shipping line was looking for volunteers to take the ship over to Greece, have a few days there whilst the formalities were completed and then be flown home by the company.

The Chef had apparently informed me at the time that he wasn't going as he already had another ship lined up which meant reluctantly he was going to have to spend the next 3 months cruising the Caribbean. What a hard life!

I must have told him that I was going over to Greece on its final trip and thought no more of it. He left the ship shortly after whilst I was 'working by'.

I didn't however go on the trip to Greece and subsequently signed up for another ship. The Chef had obviously been unaware of this fact which explained his surprise at seeing me in *Grantham*'s yard.

He had by now recovered his composure and started to explain the reason for his discomfort upon seeing me.

He informed me that on the trip to its new home in Greece, the ship had lost steerage and sunk in the notorious Bay of Biscay and all of the crew had been lost.

All of the crew on previous trips knew that the ship had a steering problem and that the Second Engineer who had completed many trips, was aware of how to deal with it. It was one of those idiosyncrasies but on a larger scale that we have all encountered in life whereby when something goes wrong, we know how to fix it by giving a kick or some such like.

A bit like computers or smart phones for example, if nothing else works switch off and back on again to clear the fault.

According to the Chef's account the ship had hit a heavy sea in the Bay and as the regular second engineer had declined to take the ship to Greece, the new engineer was unaware of the steering problem and how to fix it.

Once a ship loses steerage in a heavy sea the outcome is almost inevitable

The Chef genuinely believed that I went down with the ship. I explained that I too had received a better offer and obviously didn't go on its last journey.

This happened back in the early 1960's and as I have previously said there were no mobile phones, internet etc. and information generally was only obtained by word of mouth.

Lloyds Register of Shipping was the only real way of knowing what was happening to our shipping fleet and that was generally the means by which friends and family knew when a ship was due back into its home port.

This as I recall was by Lloyds advertising in I believe the Evening Standard, when a ship was imminently due to dock. It only appeared for one day if my memory serves me right. If your friends or family missed it on that particular day, there was no knowing until you actually returned home.

After exchanging stories for a while the Chef returned to the factory's kitchen and as he was an agency worker didn't return to *Grantham*'s again. It wasn't his fault but what he had told me about the sinking of the ship played on my mind for a considerable time after, but life moves on.

I retold this story many times to people over the following years and it was to be nearly 40 years later before I discovered the truth about the '*sinking of the ship*'.

Whilst I have been using the internet since the late 1990's, the comprehensive information we now have available to us was not widespread until at least the early to mid- 2000's, as more and more people could see the benefits and be willing to share information.

Bing and Google were in their infancy and what we now take for granted was just a fantasy until the 90's.

It may seem strange now but for years the majority of people were sceptical and were wary about embracing the new technology. It must have been the same for many people before home telephones and televisions were commonplace. The internet has transformed all of our lives mainly for the better. The challenge however is how to now harness the technology for good and not evil.

An internet search eventually revealed that the ship did in fact hit heavy seas in the Bay of Biscay and lost steerage as described by the Chef but it's believed that a salvage company managed to get ropes aboard to allow it to be towed to safety thus thankfully prevent any loss of life.

Sometime after this meeting with the chef in Basildon, Lin's mum had contacted her about a possible mutual exchange back to Romford. The tenant of a house there apparently had a thriving driving school based in Basildon and wanted to move there.

As he fitted the criteria to move into the Basildon Development Corporation area, it would have been an ideal swap for him. I wasn't too keen as I liked it in Laindon, and really had no desire to move back nearer to Dagenham.

It would have meant driving back to Basildon each day to work, a chore that didn't much appeal to me. However I knew Lin was getting homesick and as she didn't drive, had to rely on me to take her back to see her parents. It would have been selfish not to have agreed to go.

Her new friend Marion and her husband Dave had recently bought a house on Canvey Island and Dave hired a van to allow us to do the move ourselves. I had noticed that Lin, whilst she didn't say anything was feeling more and more isolated at Laindon.

After the move to Canvey Island we would visit them at the weekends on a monthly basis and vice versa. They had a stream come swamp at the back of the house and Tansy their dog had taken a liking to it.

It wasn't unusual for Marion to greet us with a roll of her eyes when we arrived. This was a signal that Dave was up to his knees in water and mud trying to retrieve Tansy from the swamp.

We all found it hilarious but for some reason Dave didn't appear to feel the same. Strange how as human beings we seem to take pleasure in other peoples discomfort yet not in our own as I was shortly to discover.

The Circus had arrived in town and it was decided that I should take the girls to see it. It was in those days a real circus with animals, clowns, bands etc.

I think they enjoyed it so much that until it was over and we had returned to the car and were on our way back to Marion's that they in unison decided that they needed the toilet. As home wasn't that far away it wouldn't have normally presented a problem but we had been stuck in a queue waiting to get out of the car park so it did.

With threats of they couldn't 'hold it' I brought the car to a halt on the dual carriageway and five little girls hastily headed for the bushes.

Now here comes my discomfort. Cars were slowing down to watch me hovering outside a hedgerow and trying discreetly to encourage the girls to be as quick as possible. The sight to passing motorists of the girls emerging one by one must have looked at the very least somewhat concerning.

I was expecting to hear sirens and the two tone horns of a police car arriving at any moment. The girls thought it was very funny and giggled all the way back. I got no sympathy from Lin, Dave or Marion. In fact Dave clearly had a smirk on his face as if to say 'see how you like it!'

Dave and I regularly retreated to the local pubs of an evening to put the world to rights but we never succeeded.

Several house moves ensued over the following years for us all and we normally used our two men and a self-drive van system until the girls grew up and we managed to elicit the help of some of their boyfriends.

The decision therefore to move to Romford was made and the formalities were duly completed. The house we had at Laindon was new and thus needed very little decoration. Romford however was relatively old and unlike Laindon had no central heating. Nevertheless we felt the move would give us more permanency and moving schools for the girls would be better now than in a few years' time.

This turned out to be the case as both Julie and Caron subsequently spent most of their school years there. Unfortunately there was a lot to do in the 'new house' but we had a large garden and good neighbours.

We never had a bad word with them in all the years we lived there. In fact all of the neighbours became friends to us so life was pretty good there.

Renovating the house was taking up quite a lot of time and the travelling back and forwards to Basildon to work was becoming more and more of a chore. I had survived a good run at *Grantham*'s and didn't want to get greedy.

Ben wasn't surprised when I told him I was leaving but was of course disappointed as I had paid him a lot of money during our time together.

Ironically and I will explain why in a moment, after giving the manager *Brian* my notice, he also surprised me by saying and I think quite genuinely that he would miss me. Now *Brian* had never been involved in myself and *Ben*'s tickles, and to the best of my knowledge was as straight as they came.

I was therefore extremely surprised after being given an order to take the lorry and clear out one of the stores which was about to close down. I was given no collection notes and just told that I was to simply collect as much of the merchandise as I could get on the van, which I did.

Upon returning to the factory and pulling onto the loading bay I opened the doors and showed *Brian* a full vehicle of clothes and various sundry items.

There were hangers, rails, shoes, suits, top coats, shirts, slacks, hats, socks and underwear all piled up in a random fashion. Nobody at the store had been making a note of what had been put on the vehicle and on the way back it had crossed my mind to have a little '*tickle*', but I decided against it because as I have said I never got greedy and this might just be the one step too far.

Going against all that I believed in, I took the whole load back, even though I was pretty sure nobody would have noticed anything missing. The staff from the closed down shop clearly had no interest as they were about to lose their jobs anyway.

Upon seeing the amount of articles on the vehicle *Brian* started to scratch his head and asking himself where there was room for it. The factory always looked full and as I have said earlier, nobody had any chance of keeping track of it.

These were different times, no computerised stocktaking therefore everything had to be noted by hand without sufficient staff to undertake such a gargantuan task. *Brian* myself and *Ben* started to unload the vehicle and about half way through *Brian* indicated to us to stop and have a break.

Now this is where the irony came in. *Brian* said he had run out of room to put the remainder of the clothes still on the lorry. There was almost half the load left on board.

I said quite casually to him, 'I've got somewhere to put it' and laughed, thinking he would just think I was joking but he immediately came back with 'WHERE'?

Somewhere safe if you know what I mean I replied. He said 'I don't want any more of it in the factory, but I wouldn't mind a few of the suits that are still on the vehicle'. I asked him, 'seriously *Brian*, do you want me to lose it' to which he replied 'if you've got somewhere to take it, it's all yours'.

He told *Ben* to go with me to help unload it but I declined, saying that I did not want anyone to know where I was taking it. That wasn't the real reason though it was in case it was a trap. I did not want *Ben* involved.

Had I have been under suspicion at all and I had helped myself on my way back to the factory from the store, I wouldn't have had any defence but because *Brian*, a part of management had allowed me to take the goods, this would have been entrapment, which in itself was illegal even in those days.

To be on the safe side though, I thought it better to keep *Ben* out of it.

My immediate next door neighbours at Laindon had sold lots of extras for me when I lived there, so I immediately headed for their place. Fortunately they were at home so we offloaded there. All of the time *Ben* and I had been careful when *Brian* had been around only to find out he was as bad as us. You couldn't make it up could you?

Once we had moved Lin found herself a job in a hairdresser's a bus ride away from our new home. By now I had left *Grantham*'s and was again doing agency work. Whilst she was there I was sent to work at a scaffold company just opposite her salon.

It was whilst in conversation with a customer that Lin told him that I was working across the road on a casual temporary basis for a scaffold company but was looking for a permanent driving job.

What a small world. The customer turned out to be the owner of the said scaffold company. Upon his return to the yard he offered me a job as his regular driver was about to go off sick for a few months. I immediately accepted and again compensation was paid to the agency for my services.

I had been doing driving jobs for a very long time which necessitated having '*tickles*' for most of the time so in some ways I was pleased that I was going to get a steady, relatively good wage without the stress of thieving, after all there could be nobody who wanted to buy stolen scaffolding. Could there?

Let's just say I spent many hours in Lin's mum's garage being supplied with copious amounts of tea whilst using paint stripper to get the paint off scaffold tube and fittings. Each scaffold company had its own identifying colour so it had to be removed before selling on. Enough said!

DEMENTIA

I didn't see it at first in my mum as the symptoms with hindsight hadn't manifested themselves until probably as early as the mid 1980's. Sam use to tell me on a regular basis that Daisy would go out and leave the oven hobs on, which fortunately were electric and not gas.

She would have been in her mid- 70's and I mistakenly thought it was just old age starting to take its toll, as it does with us all. I say mistakenly, but in fairness to myself I couldn't have known anything different.

The forgetfulness became worse over the next few years but dad seemed to be coping. I was working and had my own family and problems to deal with however I still managed to get into see them as often as I could. Fortunately my job allowed me to be relatively flexible in my work schedule.

They didn't see too much of my eldest brother Fred and the next eldest John lived with his wife Marian and son in Norfolk.

Dad appeared to handle Daisy and they seemed to chug along in their own bickering way. This was to stop in 1995 when their and my world was turned upside down.

John had a van driving job for a company near his home in Norfolk. His journeys necessitated him having to drive into London quite frequently so he took the opportunity when he could to call into their home in Dagenham.

Whilst visiting them on one particular day, as he got down from his van, his leg gave way under him.

His company sent a driver down the next day to collect him and the van.

We all paid little attention to this, as we thought he had just twisted something. I was quite close to John and obviously kept in touch through his wife Marian as to his well-being. Marian had been only a few years older than me when she met and subsequently married John so we had an affinity throughout her life.

Lin, the girls and I spent many weekends enjoying the slower pace of life that Norfolk had offered. As we all know there are certain times in your life that events stun you so much that you can remember exactly where you were when tragedy strikes.

John had been taken into Norwich and Norfolk hospital and tests were undertaken to establish the cause of his leg giving way beneath him. It was obviously more serious than was first thought.

Marian gave me regular updates as John had now been kept in for several weeks. I was becoming increasingly concerned and decided to go up to Norfolk.

For whatever reason and I know not why, I decided not to tell Marian I was going. The only thing I can recall about the journey was that the car had overheated on the way there but I was so desperate I just kept going in the hope that it would get me to the hospital.

John had various spells throughout his life when it was necessary to have to go into hospital, the reasons why I was never quite sure of. Marian always explained it as just regular check- ups and as John always seemed healthy, I thought no more of it.

This time I knew instinctively that it was different. My fears were confirmed as soon as I set eyes on him. He was a shell of the man that was my brother. I had seen cancer in my family many times and this was no different.

We just talked normally as if nothing had happened but I knew then that life would never be the same again.

Marian arrived at visiting time, but if she was surprised to see me, she never let it show. I was due to go back to Hong Kong to visit friends in a few weeks' time but I knew at that moment I would not be going.

Whilst having a coffee Marian told me as gently as she could that John had secondary cancer and that he was having radiotherapy and chemotherapy to try and contain it. She was trying to be kind and give me hope but I could see with my own eyes that unless a miracle drug was found within the next few weeks, the likelihood of John making it was very slim.

I was devastated, as was she. John had already said he wasn't going to have any more radiotherapy as the side effects were too nauseating.

I went home that same day but knew at the time that it was only to notify my bosses that I would be taking annual leave for a while to allow me to spend time with John in his final weeks of life.

This would also give Marian and my nephew a break, knowing there would always be someone there.

John passed away in a hospice in May 1995. I was there all night with him until he died the following morning. Marian and his son arrived shortly after.

Whilst sitting there alone with him that night, I was half watching West Ham playing on the TV, when John, who had been in a coma, started to try and speak. I immediately called the nurse and explained this to her and that West Ham had been our team since we were kids. She told me she thought he was agitated because he could hear the match.

Sam and Daisy knew he was ill but had no idea how ill as John had forbidden us to tell them. Whilst I wasn't sure this was the right thing to do, I respected his wishes.

Fred had been up to the hospice previously and intended to return in a day or so. I rang him and told him of John's passing. Fred was the oldest and should have been the one to tell them and although I wanted to do it, I felt he could do it better than me anyway.

I wouldn't have got back to Dagenham until very late that day and was both mentally and physically exhausted. I hadn't slept for probably 48 hours. I took up Fred's offer to tell them, for which I will be eternally grateful.

I spoke to him the following day after I had a fitful night's sleep and as expected was told Daisy took it very badly. Sam was just very quiet. I cannot imagine how that must have been for them.

By the time I saw them, Daisy had calmed down and they were both glad that I had been present at John's passing.

At these times the sequence of events is unclear and has become cloudy with time. The body's defence mechanism I should imagine is the reason for this but the one thing that does stand out in my mind was going into the then Co-op store at Tiptree to buy a few groceries on my way back from Norfolk as I knew that as I had not been at home for a while there would be no food in the house.

After placing the items on the conveyor belt and pushing the trolley to the end ready to put the items in after paying for them, one of the staff pointed out that I had left a packet of ham in the trolley. She wasn't implying that I was trying to avoid paying for them, just that I had not noticed. Perhaps the pained look on my face was there for her to see. Strange though that it is a vivid innocuous memory which has stayed with me ever since.

As much as one can after such a loss, things had to get back to normality, so that life can go on.

I returned to work and tried to get in to see Daisy and Sam as much as possible. Christmas 1995 came and went without dwelling too much on the pain we were all feeling.

Work is a subtle antidote for loss and I probably worked harder in that period than at any other time in my life.

Sadly through no fault of our own Lin and I had divorced some years earlier but we were still in touch after the initial trauma of splitting up.

Lin had a new partner but she was supportive through John's passing as was my new partner. Lin often popped into Daisy and Sam's to ensure they were okay, as I did to her mum Bette.

The New Year came and went and we all hoped that 1996 was going to be better than 1995 for obvious reasons.

Lin was working but had a few health problems, nothing too serious we had thought. I had settled into a small cottage near Burnham in Essex and whilst it was pokey, I enjoyed living there. Although on a main road it was quiet and allowed me some solace after John's death.

I knew Lin had been having routine tests after suffering from stomach pains for several months. The doctor apparently had told her to go away and have a good holiday.

It wasn't to be.

The girls turned up unexpectedly at the cottage in the spring of 1996 and told me that Lin had cancer and that it had spread.

To see the pain on their faces was heart breaking. She became increasingly unwell and naturally the girls tried as hard as they could to keep her spirits up.

I visited Lin's home on one particular day to stay with her whilst her partner got on with some local business and didn't want her left alone.

I don't think this was the reason I had been asked to go. I had known Lin since we were teenagers and seeing her withdrawn and thin left me in no doubt as what was to come. I may be wrong but I think both Julie and Caron thought she didn't know it was terminal but she did.

We talked as much as we could and both said sorry to each other.

The nature of this filthy indiscriminate disease has a pattern like no other. I had seen the same stages of decimation up close less than a year before. I assured Lin that I would be there when needed. The timeline of her illness has gone into the fog of my memory, as the brain doesn't fully function at times like this.

I now had to tell Sam and Daisy and inflict more pain so soon after the loss of their son. Sam doted on Lin and I knew it was going to be difficult but the girls helped me to tell them. They did their mum proud after the dark days that were to follow.

All of the family rallied round and in Lin's final days she couldn't have wished for more love around her.

Julie, Caron, Lin's partner Peter and I took turns in sitting with Lin through the final nights of her life.

In the early hours of the morning in April I heard Lin start to go so we said our goodbyes before she went.

The following days, weeks and months were so hard for us all but none more so than for Bette and the girls.

I can't even start to imagine how the loss of a son or daughter would feel.

AS I WALK THROUGH THE VALLEY OF THE SHADOW OF DEATH

Cancer is that evil. The only way to beat it is to try to keep going.

Caron probably doesn't remember, but she said on that awful day to me, 'will the pain get better'? I could only tell her it will get easier. I don't think it does though. I said it to protect because that's what dads do.

Whilst nobody probably wanted to go to work in those dark days I personally found it helped. At least your mind gets the chance to think of other things apart from death all of the time. I watched the pain the girls were enduring and as any parent knows, you feel helpless. You can just be there, that's all anybody can do.

It is a struggle just writing this down and after almost a quarter of a century it feels as if it has only just happened.

Grief cannot be analysed as it is the price we pay for love in any of its forms, be it family, lovers or friends. Life has to continue and we can only hope for some respite from the gut wrenching heartache that death inflicts upon us.

There was to be no respite however, as a couple of months later Sam was taken into hospital and subsequently diagnosed with terminal bowel cancer. He was a very private man and said very little about it.

He was fully aware what was happening and I didn't have to tip toe around the inevitability of the outcome. His main concern was about Daisy and how she was going to cope. I tried as best I could to assure him so he would not waste his energy worrying about her as I knew I would try to take care of her despite her dementia deteriorating.

She was My mum.

He never came out of hospital and I stayed with him in his final days. I had left him one evening when he appeared to be coming to the end of his life as I wanted to go home after days spent at the hospital to get a change of clothes and grab a few hours' sleep in my own bed, to enable me to care for and be with him at the very end.

It was very late at night and the nurses who were extremely kind to us both throughout the ordeal, had made him comfortable for the night. I knew I was going to need my strength to help him out of bed to be able to go to the toilet over the next couple of days. He was a very proud man and didn't want his dignity taken from him by having to use bedpans.

I waited until he appeared to go to sleep, kissed him on the forehead and said goodnight, saying I would see him first thing in the morning.

I never saw him alive again. The next morning on the way to hospital, the ward sister phoned me to say he had passed away in the night.

When I had left the previous evening he appeared to be asleep and I had noticed a small tear run down his cheek but had no idea of its significance at the time.

Whilst relaying the news of his passing to my sister- in-law Marian the next day, it was she who said it was probably his way of saying goodbye that evening and not put me through having to go through any more in the following days. I will never know but choose to believe she was right, if for no other reason than to ease my conscience for going home that night.

He was My dad.

I don't really remember much about the following days, or come to that, weeks and months. I can only remember feeling numb and I wasn't really in this world. Fortunately on my return to work I remember Keith, one of my colleagues, telling everybody with whom I came into contact with, to keep their distance as he believed I had the grim reaper following me around.

I am glad he said it, as it appeared to jolt me back into reality and able to function again. I don't think I had grieved properly after what had happened over the last 14 months and was surprised at my ability to cope.

Probably, because I had so many things to think of worrying about how the girls were coping, Daisy's worsening dementia and holding down a job which seemed to become ever more difficult each day.

I have subsequently watched many television programmes about dementia and heard many doctors giving opinions on the symptoms and causes of the illness, but the only people who really know about it emotionally are those who have to live with it.

It is a very difficult illness to quantify. It has no pattern. Most illnesses do. In the latter stages it needs 24 hour assistance to be given to the patient.

24 hour care is something that no individual person should undertake and should I succumb to this debilitating illness I do not want to be looked after by my family. I want to go into a care home despite this having its own pitfalls.

I know from my own experience that it will ruin any personal relationship between a carer and the patient. Dementia is an illness that defies reason.

I could ask Daisy a question and she may get it right first time but if I asked her the same question again within seconds, she would probably get it wrong.

It isn't just about forgetfulness.

It is so complex that finding a cure is going to be one of the major problems for us in the 21st century. The doctors I am sure will find the causes and know some already but the cure will be much more difficult. With longevity of life, which of course is a wonderful thing, more people are likely to suffer from the illness.

Daisy became progressively worse and whilst she continued to live in her own home after Sam died, she was gradually becoming more of a danger to herself.

We complain quite rightly that the standard of care the State gives to people with dementia is abysmal but we are so lacking of knowledge and how to handle the illness that without radical change on how to deal with it nothing will improve.

I honestly believe that until people who have experienced dementia close up are trained specifically and solely in this area are employed as carers we will continue to swim against the tide.

Unfortunately despite the efforts of many experienced, well meaning, caring individuals, there will never be the political will to deal with the problem adequately and we will just continue to expect loved ones to cope. Much more funding is needed but it's not the only answer.

Most physical injuries we can and rightly do put a lot of effort into dealing with and finding resolutions but how to care for people with dementia we appear to put too few resources into.

After years of hassling the local authority and having to deal with ' just out of college' social workers who had no idea how to deal with Daisy and saw her just as a training device I finally managed to get her into a local council care home which was brilliant for her.

I have nothing but praise for the care she received there and could not have asked for more. Despite living a two way trip of 100 miles from Dagenham, I tried to get in to see her 2 to 3 times a week but as the illness progressed she had very little idea who I was.

If people can and want to care for their loved ones who suffer from dementia they of course should be able to but no one person on their own should try. A carer must have respite and be helped by at least 2 other people within every 24 hour period otherwise not only the patient will suffer but the carers as well. An individual should not have to give up their job or career to do so.

Work is what makes us humans. Caring should be a respected, well paid career and not treated as 'a zero hours, can't get anything else job.' At the present time we have a Tory government who continue to boast that they have a record of high employment but fail to admit that full time employment use to be considered as a 40 hour week.

Whereas we use to have one person doing the 40 hour week job, we now have 4 people doing 10 hours a week doing the same job and the politicians try to justify it by saying that many people enjoy it as it gives them flexibility.

Try telling that to somebody trying to bring up a family.

CAN I DO THAT AGAIN?

In the late 1970's I started work for a Group Training Association, a private company which was Government subsidised to enable people who were out of work to train to become a Heavy Goods or Public Service Vehicle Licence Holder.

This helped them to obtain alternative work and as we were in another recession many people were being made redundant. My job was to teach them to learn both out on the road and in the classroom as many aspects of the Transport Industry as possible in the short time available to them.

Many companies were going into liquidation and insufficient funds were being put into the Road Transport Industries' coffers and consequentially not as many drivers were being sent to us for training. Ironically some of the other instructors and I were then also made redundant.

It was on one of my final days in this employment that my trainee had failed to react quickly enough to a car braking in front of us. There were always two trainees in the cab at any one time and the force of me having to engage the 'the dead man' handbrake threw the trainee in the passenger seat violently forward.

There was thankfully no collision with the vehicle in front so no injuries were sustained except for the trainee passenger complaining shortly thereafter of neck pain.

As we were in Holloway Road in North London at the time I decided to err on the side of caution and take him to the nearest hospital to get him checked over.

Initially I didn't recognise the familiar face sitting in the NHS wheelchair directly opposite me in Whittington Hospital A&E but it quickly became clear that he knew me.

Tommy Czerski wheeled himself over and started to chat as if it had been yesterday since we had last met. It had in fact been about seventeen years since we had last spoken on the *Avalon*.

At that time I would only have been a seventeen year old boy and Tommy could have been forgiven for not recognising me as the 34 year old man I had now become.

The physical changes in that time were immense in me but the facial change had remained almost indiscernible as I had always looked old for my age.

I had been drinking in pubs without any questions being asked since I was 13 years old. The disadvantages though were that I had difficulty in riding on buses with a child's ticket.

As *Tommy* had been in his twenties in the 1960's when we had first met life had been kinder to him than could be expected as he appeared to have hardly aged.

He greeted me warmly and explained that he had tripped and twisted his ankle at work hence the need of the wheelchair. The registrar had decided that it would be prudent to have the whole leg x-rayed.

Tommy and I entered into a dialogue about our lives since last seeing each other. He signalled to a young man who had accompanied him to the hospital to join us. Apparently he was *Tommy*'s partner's nephew who had begrudgingly given him a lift

After nodding a curt hello he made no attempt to enter into conversation.

Most people would have at least had the manners to give the impression he wanted to hear about *Tommy*'s past. He was one of those people who I took an instant dislike to. *Tommy* was an effervescent character and this man was not somebody you would think he would have anything in common with.

For no reason at all this man unsettled me. Perhaps he was just naturally dour.

Tommy was at the present time working for one of his relatives in North London who had a recruitment company specialising in the recruitment of personnel for several large companies currently engaged in building projects throughout London.

His job was to bring over personnel from other countries to work within the industry. The work was hard and the hours long but it was also very lucrative.

At the time I was waiting for redundancy so he immediately offered me the chance of a job as a thank you for my corroboration on the day of the robbery on the *Avalon* back in the '60's. He obviously hadn't forgotten and it appeared it had meant more to him at the time than it did to me.

The work would be mostly in London which did not appeal to me as I had no wish to commute anymore so I politely declined his offer.

He told me he had many contacts in the industry and was sure he would be able to find me something suitable. Before he had chance to explain a porter arrived to take him for an x-ray.

He gave me a phone number on which to contact him and said that we shouldn't leave it another 17 years before meeting up again but for one reason or another I never got round to it.

It had been good to see him especially as I had lost contact with many other former shipmates from those heady days in the sixties.

My trainee was subsequently checked over and a soft neck collar fitted just to be on the safe side.

THE AIRSHIP'S MAIDEN FLIGHT

I had always managed to find employment of one sort or another and this time was no different.

Sometime previously I had answered an advertisement in the Daily Telegraph I think, for applications for suitable people to become Department of Transport Driving Test Examiners at various locations throughout the country.

Much to my surprise I was invited to take a test drive by one of the Department's Supervising Examiners. For some reason or another I have always remembered that test was in my car and that I had met the Examiner in the car park at Loughton Tube Station.

I only mention it because I clearly remember an innocuous fact like this which happened nearly forty years ago but can't remember incidents from yesterday at times. I think the dementia must be kicking in.

Some months later I was invited to appear before a selection board at Lambeth Bridge House which was then the department's HQ in Central London. I don't remember much about the interview itself only that the waiting area for prospective candidates had been packed.

I think the reason for my lack of recall of the substance of it was because there had been so much time in between doing the test drive and the actual interview.

I was now working full time and earning quite good money and my thoughts at the time would probably have been that if they needed months in between test drives and interviewing applicants, how long, even if you were successful, would it take to actually start work for them.

Lo and behold a few months later I received the official On Her Majesty's Service brown envelope and to my surprise was informed that I had been successful and that a place had been earmarked for me at the Civil Service Training Establishment at Cardington in Bedfordshire.

Whilst I quite naturally took pride in the achievement of passing the Board, the amount of time the whole process had taken left a bitter sweet taste in my mouth. By now Lin and I had settled into a comfortable lifestyle and I was reluctant to commit to taking up the position.

The original application had been Lin's idea and she seemed keen for me to go to Cardington despite the substantial drop in wages this would entail. Secretly, though she never said it, I think she was proud to say her husband was going to be a Driving Test Examiner. A respected job at that time. Few people have respect for anything now.

I wasn't sure that I felt the same but in fairness to her as she had put up with a lot from me regarding unstable work periods in the past I decided to give it a go. I will always be eternally grateful to her as it opened up doors and allowed me to see things I would never have otherwise seen.

To the best of my knowledge Cardington had been an airfield used by the military in the Second World War. It consisted of large aircraft hangars and later became a base for airship storage.

Without being melodramatic we genuinely didn't know who we could be talking to as my new found friend Richard and I were to find out.

Richard was always cracking jokes and taking the piss and it could have really backfired sometime later on in the course whilst watching the national news on TV in one of the lounges.

On the day in question TV cameras had been filming a piece about the inaugural flight of an Airship which was taking place from the hangar at Cardington situated in the Establishment grounds.

The TV presenter who I think was from Anglia News but I could be wrong, had just completed the interview with the pilot when Richard just came out with a comment about the pilot being 'a real scruffy bastard' and who would want to fly with him?

As God is my witness, the person sitting next to Richard said to him 'I couldn't agree more young man. I had no idea the cameras were going to be here today, so I did not bother to get out of my overalls'

If anybody had a camera they would have got a marvellous picture of all our mouths wide open at the sight of the pilot sitting there, still in his overalls.

He took it in a good spirit (or two) and we all sat chatting with him aided by a few whiskies for the next hour or so. There was no internet in those days and only a few TV channels, so the chance to talk to somebody new relieved the boredom.

Richard was unfortunately his own worst enemy and despite serving as a soldier in Ireland in the Troubles he had a childish naivety about him.

He was conscientious to a fault but sometimes allowed his judgement to be clouded by it. There were times as in all walks of life when it would have been more prudent to shrug shoulders and accept that whatever would be would be. Que sera sera.

It just wasn't in his character. He was about to conduct the 'emergency stop' exercise when as was customary before moving off, he glanced over his right shoulder to ensure there was no traffic immediately following the car and noticed that a bag of white powder had fallen out of the candidate's bag and onto the back seat.

This unsettled Richard and remained on his mind until pulling up outside the test centre at the conclusion of the test. By now he had convinced himself that the powder was cocaine.

Now here is where it got difficult for him. In effect driving test examiners have no other duty than to conduct a test so essentially they do not exist as they are observers not instructors. It may seem odd but nonetheless true.

What anybody has in their car should be of no interest to the examiner but in this case Richard despite having no knowledge of what the white powder was had already decided it was his duty to be public spirited and inform the police of his suspicions.

Making an excuse to the candidate that he had left some of his paperwork in the office he asked him to wait in the car for a few moments whilst he retrieved it.

There were no mobile phones then so he went back into the test centre and phoned the local police station which at this particular centre was only about 200 yards away. They assured him they would respond immediately.

Within minutes of returning to his candidate's car there were at least 2 cars and five officers in attendance.

Most examiners upon returning to the test centre would merely have added their suspicions to a report after the test had finished.

Not Richard though.

The powder turned out to be corn flour. Apparently the candidate worked in a restaurant nearby and just had it in his bag to take into work after his test.

The Department weren't at all pleased.

Richard being Richard had his lighter moments though. He could even enthral seasoned, cynical examiners with his amusing stories of his exploits.

On one particular test he had given instructions to an Oriental gentleman before proceeding with the 'emergency stop' exercise that 'when given the signal he would like him to bring the vehicle to a stop immediately and under full control, as though a child had run off the pavement.'

The candidate moved off and just as Richard was about to check over his shoulder before giving the signal, the man applied his brakes. A child, unseen by Richard because he was checking behind, had run into the road.

The man looked at Richard enquiringly and said in his Chinese accent,

“How you do that”

He had obviously genuinely thought Richard had trained a child to run into the road to enable him to do the ‘emergency stop’.

It has to be remembered that the Driving Test was and still is one of the most important days of most peoples’ lives.

It was a difficult career then to get access to but I went through all the test drives, interview boards and Cardington mainly to prove I could do it but I knew it wasn’t for me, however it was reasonable pay and reasonable hours so I stuck with it for some years until the chance arose to leave and do something different.

HONG KONG

It was whilst at Cardington that I met Aldo a Civil Servant from Hong Kong who subsequently became a lifelong friend.

Aldo and I kept in touch by letter and the occasional phone call over the next few years until his return to the UK to visit Chinese friends sometime in the late 1980's.

He came to stay with me for a while and it was as if it had been only days since we had seen each other.

There were more frequent visits by him over the following years as he and his wife Daisy wanted to have their daughter Ava educated in England.

The visits became gradually longer and we spent times looking at schools locally and in the university cities. I managed to fit in annual leave to accommodate him in his search and we were able to spend plenty of time with each other.

He was and still is a very generous man and as I would not take any money for petrol and his keep whilst he was with me, he would try and buy me expensive gifts wherever we went.

Perhaps it was my upbringing but I couldn't take anything as I felt that he would then be buying my friendship and that wasn't necessary. We were already friends and whilst our cultures were very different we rubbed along together with the same sense of humour we had forged at Cardington.

Regardless he still whenever he came over would bring me and my family loads of gifts of clothes and jewellery and also try to give me cash which I would not accept. He had made many good investments over the years and was a relatively wealthy man. Nonetheless I just couldn't take cash from him, it wasn't in my nature.

It needed many years for me to understand that it was the Chinese culture to give presents to their friends and nothing was expected in return.

To this day he still brings a suitcase full of presents whenever he comes over.

Eventually after consultation with Daisy in Hong Kong, they decided upon the school they wanted Ava to study in was situated in Cambridge. After the paperwork had been completed with the headmistress he returned home but not before one essential errand had been completed.

There was very little he could not buy in Hong Kong but Doc Marten boots were all the rage for the kids there but were very difficult and exorbitantly expensive to buy. I had found a shop in Grays, Essex where they were easily obtainable in a variety of sizes.

Off we trotted to buy a couple of pair to send to Ava, or so I thought.

Aldo asked the shopkeeper in the town centre if he had about 30 pairs in varying sizes in stock. The man looked at him in amazement as if it was a joke and looked to me as if to act as an interpreter as he thought Aldo perhaps meant three pairs. I assured him that if Aldo said thirty he meant thirty and that if he wanted Aldo to confirm it in several other languages it wouldn't be a problem for him.

The shopkeeper thought all of his Christmases had come at once and immediately ordered one of his staff to go to the stock room to check for availability.

I explained to Aldo that to send 30 boxes of boots to Hong Kong by post from the UK would be very expensive but he told me not to worry as he would take them on the plane with him.

I saw no reason to argue with him. He was a very shrewd man and had already worked out the prestige if not profit margin on each pair of boots.

They for some reason were like gold dust in Hong Kong and no doubt before his flight had touched down they all would have been placed with the eager recipients.

Whilst he didn't generally dabble in this sort of enterprise as he had made his money in financial and property investment, he still had an eye for a small bargain. It was unusual for goods to be worth buying in the UK for resale in Hong Kong as it was almost always the other way around.

This was demonstrated several years later when 'Furbies' were the craze at Christmas time in the UK. Several of my friends just could not get hold of them anywhere in the shops but Aldo had no trouble and sent me a dozen or so by post and would accept no payment for them.

Back to the boots and after successful negotiations with the shopkeeper there we were with an enormous ball of string sitting in my daughter's flat in Grays tying the boxes up securely for their trip to the other side of the world.

Fortunately Aldo travelled light which allowed us to get them all in the car on his return trip to Heathrow.

Sometime after his return home I received a letter from Aldo and Daisy asking if I would be guardian to Ava whilst she attended school at Cambridge which I was only too willing to be.

I was however not prepared to accept the financial rewards that were offered but undertook the task as their friend and only on that condition.

The next time I saw him was when he and Daisy returned with Ava to commence her studies.

Understandably Ava was not happy with the situation as she was a young girl of perhaps eleven or twelve years of age having to settle in an alien country for the foreseeable future without the comfort of her family or friends. Whist Daisy told me Ava could speak English she did not have the confidence to do so in front of me and it was some time before she actually tried.

She spent most of the short school holidays at the school and she had started to make friends with other Chinese girls there but generally went home to Hong Kong for the long vacations.

Aldo would sometimes come over out of school term time to see her but she was now a teenager with all of the inherent problems that would bring.

Quite naturally she didn't want to spend her holidays with two what in her eyes were old men and much preferred staying at her new friend's houses in the short breaks.

There was however one occasion when it wasn't possible for Ava to do so in the holidays and as she was becoming a young woman I didn't think it appropriate for her and a friend to stay on their own with me so with Aldo and Daisy's permission she stayed for some of the time with Julie and some with Caron.

She pestered Caron to be allowed with Daisy's permission to go to London with her young friend for the day and promised to stick to the return home time she was given but needless to say didn't.

They were so late in returning that Caron was increasingly concerned and eventually because of their youth and being alone in a strange to them capital city, she informed the local police. We had of course to tell Daisy and upon their eventual return Ava had to incur the wrath of both Caron and Daisy.

Teenagers, who'd 'av 'em?

Aldo however continued to make frequent visits to the UK and often before returning home would try and encourage me to go back to Hong Kong with him. I had travelled extensively around the world in my teenage years and had never been there but for various reasons the time then was not right.

He was starting to buy property in the UK as an investment for Ava's future and we occasionally went looking together. He eventually bought a flat in the East End of London and several other purchases followed over the ensuing years.

In 1993 British Airways were doing a much reduced rate offer for flights around the world and Pauline and I decided that we would make the trip to see Aldo and Daisy.

After consultation with them they asked us to go and stay for the Chinese New Year which we readily agreed to.

My friend Dee's son David was studying in Hong Kong in 1993 and had stayed for a short period with Aldo. As Julie had also been invited to go and stay with them which she did whilst David was there, we decided to leave it for a while to give them a break from visitors for a short time.

We arrived in Hong Kong after scarily appearing to hit the roof tops of the buildings below, a sight no longer possible to see as passengers no longer arrive via the old airport of Hong Kong.

There was also the added problem of planes overshooting the runway and dropping straight into the harbour. Whilst there we actually saw one aircraft that had done so, not the incident just the aftermath which left it nosedived into the water with its tail end still clear to see.

The problem fortunately was eradicated when a new state of the art airport was built elsewhere sometime later.

It was mid-day local time when we touched down and the smell emanating from the city was indescribable once the plane door had been opened. It was a real culture shock which the obvious long flight had only exacerbated.

After completing the routine formalities we stepped out into the warm air to be greeted by Aldo.

He immediately rushed us off to a restaurant to eat but neither of us was hungry as our body time clock was out of skew from the long flight so he took us to his flat to be able to relax for a while.

Aldo had already made plans for the coming days to take me to meetings with the local dignitaries to introduce me to them as his English colleague. It was still prestigious for Chinese people to have friends from what was still then 'the mother country'.

Until the territory was handed back to the Chinese government a few years later the people of Hong Kong still considered themselves to be a part of the UK.

Unfortunately as Daisy was still working as a teacher she was unable initially to take Pauline around the multitude of shops for which Hong Kong is famed.

The place at the time was a very male cultured society and Aldo had failed to see that neither Pauline nor I wanted to spend our time apart for the whole three weeks we intended to stay. It was after all supposed to be holiday.

He had not meant any offence by trying to drag me around many lunches and dinners meeting his colleagues all over the island on our own. It was just the culture. Women and men mainly did their own thing and to a degree led very different lives.

I explained my concerns to him upon our return back to the flat on the very first day after our arrival. Whilst she did not show it, understandably Pauline was very upset. She had been left alone in a strange flat in a strange city and coupled with the jet lag felt underwhelmed with what after all was supposed to be the trip of a lifetime.

She never complained but I assured her that it wasn't my idea of a holiday either and I would diplomatically convey my thoughts to Aldo. He would have to compromise if we were going to stay.

Once it was explained to him he was mortified and ensured that Pauline was part of everything we did from thereon in.

THE DRIVING TEST

Driving Test Examiners were few and far between and the sheer nature of the job entailed meeting people from all walks of life who all wanted something we could give them.

A Pass Certificate.

This would enable them to drive anywhere in the world for the rest of their lives.

Driving is something that most people want to do and that meant having to satisfy one of us that they were a competent person to drive on a public road and because everybody in the country , except for the Queen, has to undertake this test, it is inevitable that human nature will play its part.

I quickly learned that it was unwise to admit I was an examiner as it would mean either endless monologues about one or other person's own test or questioning about the myths that surrounded it.

Whenever we were asked what we did for a living the stock answer was generally we were in the Civil Service. If any further clarification was needed it was just that we shuffled paper around which satisfied most enquirers.

Most examiners were the same and whilst we took pride in doing the job to the best our ability we just did not enjoy talking about. Relatively speaking I didn't do the job for that long but still nonetheless conducted thousands of tests, each one being different.

Lin also quickly realised it was not a good idea to talk about it with most people. She was a hairdresser and had one particular young lady client who was due to take her test but had no idea that I was an examiner. We ourselves never discussed about anybody having their test, certainly not before the event.

Some days after her test the young lady went into Lin's Salon to have her hair done and the other clients in the Salon asked her how she had got on.

The young lady went into a rant about how the examiner had failed her but that it wasn't going to be the end of it. Apparently she announced that there had been three examiners in the car on her test.

One was the Chief Examiner, another being the Senior Examiner of the Test Centre the actual examiner's boss, plus the examiner himself.

The Chief Examiner and the actual examiner's boss, according to this young lady had both told her examiner to pass her as she was good but her examiner refused to do so. They both told him that unless he did he would be in trouble and assured her that the matter was going much higher and that she would be hearing from them at a later date as they intended getting the result reversed.

Now on this particular day Lin's mum had been in the Salon having her hair done and couldn't resist asking the young lady if she knew the examiner's name. She proudly pulled out the failure sheet and Bette could clearly see my signature on the bottom of the sheet.

Unbeknownst to the young lady, Lin knew quite a lot about driving tests because she had to listen to my boss and I talking about them in general terms almost every day of the working week. My boss lived only a mile or so from us and I used to give him a lift home every evening. We would stop off and collect Lin from her Salon on the way.

She frequently had to listen to clients' discussing their own or relatives driving tests about how it was all the examiner's fault but it was water off a ducks back to her but after listening to this young lady's rant Lin for some reason snapped. Possibly because some of the clients in the Salon knew me. Lin was going to have none of this tissue of lies.

After Lin had suitably read the riot act to her, the young lady never returned to the Salon again. Lin knew there were never any more than one examiner in the car at any time except if the examiner was being check tested and then there could only be one other but they could not by law talk to the conducting examiner, to the candidate, or make any comment on the test.

The examiner's decision was final and could not be overturned even by the Secretary of State for Transport.

A court could allow a re-test but only if the test had not been conducted in accordance with the Regulations. They could not reverse the decision.

This young lady was not unusual as it was easier to blame somebody else for her inability to pass the test than to admit the blame for her failure was hers alone. Never in my life have I ever heard somebody admit that their failure was of their own doing. Even me!

It is a human frailty that none of us like to admit failure.

The first few years were spent at a Test Centre where I slipped into a routine of eight tests per day five days per week. I also tested at various other test centres to cover sickness or annual leave.

Most test centres had at least one examiner prepared to travel at short notice so as to enable tests not having to be cancelled and thus causing disappointment to candidates. In fairness to the Department they detested having to cancel at short notice almost to a point of paranoia.

Examiners had the bonus of gaining experience at other centres and meeting colleagues they would otherwise rarely, if ever, see. It also enabled the Driving Test to be kept as uniform as possible throughout the country. This ensured that all candidates regardless of where they lived received as fair a test as possible.

Driving Test Examiners as such were a cynical bunch but I must say in all honesty that every one that I came into contact with tried to be as fair and impartial as was humanly possible. The same could not be said at times of some candidates.

There were various forms of emotional tactics undertaken in an effort to sway us into looking favourably upon their efforts.

The nurse who would turn up in her pristine, recently pressed uniform.

The doctor who would arrive in the waiting room with a stethoscope around his neck.

There was also the young police officer who presented himself for test in dress uniform.

The pretty girl with the short skirt who when positioned in the drivers' seat had an almost shorter skirt.

On a beautiful summers day before the start of her test one young lady had opened all of the car windows which of course was her right and then spent over half of the test with her skirt covering the upper half of her body with her undergarments clearly on view because of a gust of wind.

She had plenty of opportunity to pull the skirt back down whilst stopped at the side of the road but was so engrossed in concentration that she also failed to notice!

As Ross a friend from Wales put it in his Welsh brogue:

"I wasn't going to say anything to her boyo in case she took offence and anyway I was enjoying it too much".

Yes all really true!

Nothing surprised us.

Different times.

There was also the other extreme. One young man spent the whole of the test 'grunting' after each direction I gave to him. As the test progressed his grunts appeared to get louder and harsher as if he was becoming angry.

I had already started to think about how near I could get to the office to park at the end of the test in case he failed and I needed to make a quick exit from the car.

He was a mountain of a man!

As we progressed he started to perspire to such an extent that I was starting to be concerned about his ability to see because of the sweat running from his forehead but as he was concentrating so much I don't think he even noticed. There was no thought of wiping his brow for this youngster.

The grunting young man had thankfully given me an exceptionally good drive, in fact probably one of the best I ever had whilst testing. We pulled up at the end and I went through the formality of asking questions on the Highway Code, (the written theory test wasn't in existence then). Even his answers were 'grunt like'.

I gave him the good news and to my astonishment he burst into tears, sobbing uncontrollably.

For candidates to cry after passing was not an unusual occurrence as this was obviously a way of releasing tension on what was after all is said and done one of the most important days in a person's life.

As Examiners we had all been through the experience ourselves so we tried to keep sight of how we would have felt at the time.

It took some time for the young man to control his emotions but as we had so little time in between tests to complete the paperwork, time was at a premium and it was incumbent upon us in fairness to our next candidate to expedite ourselves from the test as quickly as possible.

I was by now an experienced enough examiner and instinct told me to give this young man a few moments to compose himself before I made my departure. He had not said a word to me throughout the test, apart from the grunts of course and I was curious to know the reason why.

The floodgates opened and he began to tell me that he was a soldier and had just come back from the Falklands after re-capturing the islands from the Argentinians. He said that for all the hardships he had endured in that war zone nobody had put him under stress as I had on that test.

I explained as gently as I could that I had not put him under pressure as I had conducted his test in the same manner as I had conducted every other test. The stress had come from within him.

It was an unwritten law that we never gave praise or made any comment to any candidate after they had passed as we did not want the person to go away thinking that they were God's gift to driving because of our comments and go and wrap their car around a lamppost.

I had never before, or never did after this test, make any comments to a candidate but I thanked him for a nice drive and congratulated him on passing his test.

A very brave young man!

This was probably the one test that I had conducted which has stayed so vivid in my mind.

I do remember a test with a young lady at the wheel attempting to do the reverse into a side road manoeuvre and lost control of the clutch and rammed into a parked car, looked at me and said **"Can I do that again?"**

Examiners despite what people think, are actually human and I had to restrain myself from saying "You want to do **THAT** again?." The thought of spending my own time in responding to the complaint letter made me resist the temptation.

Let me take a moment here to try and dispel a common myth. I have heard on countless occasions "Examiners have to fail so many people".

Utter rubbish.

We much preferred to give a Pass than a Failure as there was much less writing to do.

The Department liked it much more as well.

Or am I being too cynical?

Perhaps I will write a book on the Confessions of a Driving Test Examiner some time. Perish the thought!!!

THE NORFOLK BROADS

Sometime in the early 1980's a conversation with one particular examiner I knew from a different test centre resulted in us realising we both had a love for the 'Norfolk Broads'. His name was Clive and once again the most apt way to describe him was as a gentle giant.

Standing at over 6'4' tall and broad, which in those days was very tall he must have been a terrifying sight for candidates in the waiting room who most of I am sure prayed it wasn't their name he was going to call out.

They had no need to be alarmed though, he was a quiet, well spoken, jovial figure and I'm sure he would have put most candidates at ease. If ever a Driving Test Examiner deserved the title as most affable examiner, it would have been he.

A real gentleman.

Lin and I came to know Clive and his lovely wife Mary quite well over the following years and a visually different couple you would find it hard to imagine. Clive as I have said stood at over six feet and Maureen weighed in at about four foot six inches, if that. We all knew in the nicest way though, who was the boss.

Clive was a very knowledgeable man but Maureen would never as she would put it let him 'get above his station'. It was a lovely loving relationship but nevertheless could be comical to observe.

They enjoyed spending time together on the Norfolk Broads and in fact owned a cruiser which was moored at Dilham, a small inlet of the Broads. In conversation it transpired that they had just purchased a larger boat and his old boat which itself was 25' long was shortly to go up for sale as there was insufficient room on his berth for both boats.

I expressed an interest in buying it and so he and Maureen invited us up to Dilham to take a look. My brother lived in Norfolk and as it was our intention to go to see him anyway, we decided to make a day of it.

On a lovely Spring day we met them at their mooring which incidentally they owned, which wasn't that common as most moorings were on a 'to let' basis and few and far between.

I immediately fell in love with the place. It was idyllic.

I made Clive an offer for his older boat which he accepted. He also managed to get me a small mooring within seeing distance of theirs. It was up for let and saved me the trouble of having to find one. It was small but overhung by a large Oak tree giving us lots of shade.

All I needed to do then was to sort out how to finance it.

I had recently changed banks to an up and coming concern and they seemed eager to compete with the big banks thus offering at the time various perks.

In a relatively short time I had come to know the manager quite well.

What I am about to write the reader can be forgiven for thinking is pure fantasy but I can swear on my children's lives the crux of it really happened. It must be remembered this was over 35 years ago and applications for loans were not made online as the internet didn't exist at that time.

Loans generally had to be personally approved by the manager and for the sum of £3000 which was a tidy amount so were accompanied by an interview with him. I seemed to have an affinity with him and this fact coupled with the bank's apparent willingness to throw money at people to get them signed up resulted in a quick approval of the loan.

As the boat was to be a cash purchase from Clive, the manager readily agreed to have the full amount available to me the next day. It wasn't unusual then, as the bank transfer system as such never existed for the likes of us.

The following morning I went into the bank and watched the young lady cashier count out the money and then put it into an envelope for me. As she had been counting the cash I had the distinct feeling that she had made a mistake but I was sure if I was right it was in my favour so I am ashamed to say I said nothing.

Once home I counted it again but for some reason I had to go straight out so I decided to hide it and deal with it upon my return.

Later that same afternoon Lin received a phone call from our friendly bank manager saying whilst cashing up, the tellers had found a discrepancy of £300 in one of the tills and it was in fact the young lady who had served me whose till was short. Apparently there had been several large withdrawals from her till and he was ringing every customer in an attempt to track down the missing amount.

He explained to Lin that whilst the bank had closed, which was 3pm in those days, he only had a limited amount of time to trace the money before he would have to phone head office and that would cause problems for the cashier. At the very least the young lady may have to reimburse the bank.

He told Lin he was clutching at straws and didn't expect anybody to admit they had been overpaid, why would they?

She informed him that I wasn't at home and therefore had no idea where I had put the money but would try to get hold of me as soon as possible.

Upon my return we checked and found the extra £300 in the envelope. We decided that whilst we were under no legal obligation to give the money back because nobody was actually aware we had it anyway, we didn't want to cause problems for the young lady cashier.

At least if we told the manager he may be able cover up the discrepancy and save any grief for her as nobody except him needed to know about it. She could possibly have lost her job and at the very least her reputation as a competent teller.

Perhaps this was just my way of purging my conscience for all the thieving I had taken part in.

If the manager was prepared to help her so was I.

I phoned the Manager and told him that I had checked in the envelope and was pleased to tell him the missing £300 pound was there.

I explained it would be difficult to get to the bank this day but could return it first thing in the morning. He assured me that now he knew it was safe he could cover the mistake out of his own account until such time as I could get into the branch.

He was a young man and I got the impression that he was a relatively new Manager and if something like this had got back to Head Office it would not have been something he would want on his record. He just wasn't what most people would consider to be a Bank Manager.

In fact I saw him as bordering on 'a Jack the Lad' type or perhaps I was just looking in the mirror.

It is said that honesty is the best policy which is something up until then I had never agreed with. This incident proved to be the exception and I will tell you why.

Over the next few months I visited the bank on several occasions and whilst I saw the young lady cashier who had made the overpayment and had thanked me for my honesty, I never saw the Manager in the bank again.

A new Manager arrived sometime later but I had no reason to engage with him. I am so glad I made no attempt to introduce myself as I had not received any loan agreement to sign or any demand for monthly payments from the bank. Whilst I considered asking the young lady about the absence of the previous Manager I thought it best to let sleeping dogs lie.

It seemed as if the Bank were blissfully unaware of the loan, thankfully for me. I never heard anything about it from that day onwards. '*Lovely Jubbly.*'

I can honestly say this was '*the bank that liked to say yes*'

At the time the loan had been initially granted I must admit I found it strange that no real formalities had been undertaken. To the best of my knowledge he never checked for any sort of references, be it employer, character or previous loan history.

It must be understood that as such there were no Credit Reference Agencies unlike today where one's whole personal and financial viability can be checked at the click of a button.

Clive was summarily paid the £3000 and we purchased the boat. We kept it for several years and spent many pleasurable days on it. Our friends Dave and Marion who by now had moved to the coast also become interested in doing something similar and subsequently purchased a small day boat.

I clearly remember us taking it on a trailer to Norfolk and lowering it into the water via a slipway but I am not sure who else helped. I believe it was one of their daughter's boyfriends but I can't be certain. It remained tied up alongside us at Dilham for several summers.

Several years later after Lin and I split up, I sold it to Don a work colleague. His son was an R.A.F. Tornado Pilot and the idea was for them to spend time together on the Broads when he was on leave. He told me that whilst flying at supersonic speeds in a Tornado was exhilarating, the snail's pace of the boat had a similar effect on him.

From one extreme to another.

Unfortunately before they had time to enjoy it Don died suddenly and unexpectedly. His son then found it difficult to commit to looking after the boat so I offered to buy it back from him for the price I had sold it to his dad but unfortunately the mooring manager at Dilham, a real arsehole, told him that unless it was sold to him, the new purchaser would have to find another mooring and they are like gold dust to find on the Broads.

He knew that would be difficult and he had played on Don's son's grief, so reluctantly he had to sell it to him for a knockdown price. The greedy 'scroat 'obviously had somebody lined up to buy it.

JURY SERVICE

In the early 1980's whilst working on driving tests I was given notice to appear for jury service at the Old Bailey. I had been told by other people who had done the same that it could be very boring, especially at the Old Bailey as many people were summoned to attend but were never called for actual jury service.

I never found it to be the case and was fortunate to meet up with a man who lived in the next road to me. We had been on nodding acquaintance but the opportunity arose now to become friends. Strangely enough we were both called out of the 'pool' of jurors to adjudicate on the same trials.

The first being a case of female rape whereby the victim admitted to being a prostitute. She had for reasons that I now do not recall, said 'no' to the alleged rapist just at the point before actual penetration.

The reasons she gave for saying 'no' I do not recall but as far as I was and still am concerned, it is the point at which no further attempt at sexual intercourse should be made. Any man, as in this case who continued to try to have sexual intercourse after the word NO is spoken, is guilty of rape in my opinion regardless of the victim's profession.

Both I and my new friend who was also called Dave, were of the same opinion and subsequently voted accordingly. We were the only two that did so and because the judge accepted a majority 10-2 decision the perpetrator walked free. I wouldn't dream of questioning the jury system as it has stood us in good stead for many years but the way we chose jurors did concern me.

To be judged by our peers is quite correct and any variants from this philosophy itself causes anomalies and I do not even attempt to offer a better solution to ensure that justice is done.

To even try is fraught with danger.

Whilst deliberating on our verdict, I was astonished at the vitriol the women jurors attributed to the victim.

Whilst this occurred over 35 years ago, I can honestly say I don't believe this would be the case today. It is now and was then, the case that if a woman or come to that a man says No, it means No.

One of the women jurors actually said and I paraphrase, "you can't have sex in a mini therefore the accused rapist couldn't have been guilty". The naivety of this woman was astonishing. The accuser was being judged for her profession not for her allegation.

That day they let a rapist walk free.

I watched the police officers faces after the verdict and their incredulity was clear to see. Women who were prepared to come forward after that trial may understandably have had grave misgivings.

For hardened police officers to bring forward a case knowing the odds were clearly stacked against the accuser yet still persevered to get justice for her, was to my mind a travesty of justice caused by bigoted, naive, un-streetwise people.

My belief in the jury system and any woman's rights regardless of her occupation was dealt a large blow at that trial.

The next trial was one of armed robbery and as sure as night meets day, the perpetrators were as guilty as sin.

Dave and I had grave doubts after the previous jury farce. Fortunately our concerns were unnecessary. All defendants were unanimously found guilty.

However, one of the days at the Old Bailey I did enjoy was being given a tour of Number One Central Criminal Court. An awesome eerie sensation overcame me as it did many of the other jurors in that court.

So much criminal history!

POACHER TO GAMEKEEPER

In the mid 1980's many police forces did not have the powers or inclination to enforce the law with regard to Heavy Goods Vehicles, Public Service Vehicles and various other categories of transport. These duties mainly fell within the remit of the Department of Transport's Traffic and Vehicle Examiners whose force I joined after transferring from Driving Tests.

The job consisted of enforcing the regulations in regard to most forms of vehicles used on public roads. We were a relatively unknown breed to the public at large and as we did not generally wear uniforms it enabled us to work covertly most of the time.

The only power we didn't have but I believe now do, was to physically command vehicles to stop. However as soon as a vehicle's wheels stopped moving, our powers kicked in.

The first six months of my new posting was spent training in the field and my initial mentor was a retired Gorbals cop. For the uninitiated the Gorbals was at one time probably the most dangerous place in the UK to live or police.

It consisted of mainly council house tenements in the slums of the City of Glasgow. He was a strict disciplinarian which was understandable in view of his previous career.

He stood about 6'2" tall and was then in his early 60's. There wasn't an ounce of fat on his body. Other members of the office which consisted of mainly retired police officers, driving test examiners and men from the transport industry were wary of him and whilst behind his back he was the butt of many jokes because of his broad Scottish accent, nobody would dream of saying anything to his face.

He was aggressive by nature and rubbed many people up the wrong way but I always had a good relationship with him and remained friends until his death in 2014. After retiring from the job in the late 1980's, along with his wife he returned to his beloved Scotland.

We kept in touch and it had been my intention to go and stay with him at his home in the Scottish Isles but it wasn't to be as he died before I had chance to make the journey.

His daughter kindly sent me an album consisting of photographs and a brief outline of his life. His son had followed his footsteps into the police force and I am sure they all deeply missed him.

The album was a real eye opener for me, as along with other colleagues in the office we were completely unaware of his bravery. Whilst in the force in Scotland he had gone into and rescued a man from a burning building.

He had never mentioned it to any of us. Real heroes rarely do.

I had some good times with him and if ever in any sort of trouble, he would be the man I would want backing me up. Doing our duty may sound corny but try telling that as I had to do to a grieving mother who had lost her motorcyclist son because of a reckless Heavy Goods Vehicle driver who shouldn't even have been driving.

He had obtained his Licence by omission of facts and should not have been anywhere near a Heavy Goods Vehicle. He only had one eye thus diminishing his visibility but by failing to notify the Authorities of this fact he was issued with a Heavy Goods Vehicle Licence.

It was a small comfort to her but I had managed at least to get it taken from him as the investigations into the accident at the time had been unaware of his impairment.

Neither she nor I were criticising the findings of the investigation as they were unaware of the full facts but a mother's instinct had alerted her that things weren't as they should have been. Fortunately he wasn't going to be driving HGV's legally again.

My duties were varied and alongside traffic police officers consisted of stopping vehicles to check they were complying with the law. As I gained experience I gradually became more integrated with them and saw first- hand when they had the unenviable task of picking up the pieces after fatal accidents caused by or involving HGV or Public Service Vehicles.

Whilst the police had their own Accident Investigation Units to establish how accidents happened, their knowledge and powers at that time were limited with regards to how long drivers were allowed to drive etc. A 'Tachograph' is a device which theoretically allowed police to ascertain these facts but unfortunately their knowledge was limited and there were insufficient officers who specialised in the subject.

I spent a large part of my time in various Traffic Police garages. Large parts of the motorway network were covered by officers from these garages and at that time had very limited powers to hold vehicles for any length of time.

They had to rely on our services to assist them in prohibiting vehicles from moving. Fortunately things were changing and it was now possible for them to '*page*' me. (A now out-dated system whereby their number would come up on a small portable text like device enabling me to contact them by phone).

There was a new culture of co-operation between us as many more young Traffic officers were taking an interest in this field and starting to specialise. We all had the same goal which was to get the killer drivers and vehicles off the roads.

In the case of foreign vehicles if police detected offences they could generally only report them and let them on their way never to be seen again, so thus a pointless exercise.

Depending on the information they gave me I could get to the scene to issue a prohibition notice should the offences warrant it. An amount of trust gradually built up between me and all of the local traffic garages in my area so that every part of our area of the county had cover.

These officers whilst experienced mostly did not have the knowledge with regards to how Operators and drivers managed to evade the law. Remember I had driven HGV's for many years and knew most of the 'fiddles.'

If these officers were willing to specialise, I was willing to help them.

Traffic Examiners had powers to inspect any documents kept at any premises where they believed a goods vehicle to be kept. The police needed a search warrant to do so. Having us present enabled them to be much more adventurous.

If I came across any documentation on relevant premises which interested me, I could copy or seize it to help me with my investigation.

The introduction of the new Police and Criminal Evidence Act was bringing in radical changes within all Enforcement Agencies throughout the UK.

Before P.A.C.E. was adopted, all enforcement officers worked under what was known as 'Judge's Rules' and there was little obligation to record anything when questioning suspects. Quite frankly any record made of interviewing a suspect could be made on the back of a cigarette packet and as long as the officer confirmed that the notes were made at the time, Judges would often accept them in Court as original notes.

This was and had been the normal practice for decades but times were changing.

Under Judge's rules when an enforcement officer considered it appropriate a caution was given to a suspect as follows:

'Anything you say will be taken down and may be given in evidence.'

Under P.A.C.E this changed to:

'You do not have to say anything but it may harm your defence if you do not mention when questioned something which you may later rely on in court. Anything you do say will be taken down and given in evidence'

We now see it used on all our television programmes but at the time it was revolutionary.

Apart from a few minor tweaks this is the same caution as is still used today, some 30 plus years later.

Don't worry, just try and stay awake for a few more minutes as it is as boring for me as it is for you.

My boss, despite not being far off retirement was forward thinking and could see that radical changes were on their way and we should adapt whenever possible.

He had been a cop for most of his working life and the best way to describe him would be to visualise 'Desperate Dan' from the Dandy or Beano, I can't remember which.

He was the person everybody in the office up looked up to for advice on tachographs and the law. He had the foresight to see that things were drastically changing and that it would be my generation whose job it was going to be to implement these changes.

He had been informed by Essex Police that they were setting up a HGV Enforcement Squad and they had approached him with a view to eliciting one of his Traffic Examiners to assist their Traffic Officers who were going to undertake an Intelligence led investigation into a road haulage company.

He told me that in view of my experience in the transport industry, my ever growing knowledge of tachograph fiddling, knowledge of company law and being trained in P.A.C.E. that he would like me to be that Examiner

We had our own solicitors, unlike the police who were basically guided by the Crown Prosecution Service. Whereas the police had to seek agreement from them to go ahead with prosecutions, it was not the same for us. We as the Examiners on the ground, through our senior officers had the say on who was prosecuted. The Department after all was said and done, paying solicitors as individual entities.

He made it clear that it wasn't an order but felt it would be to everyone's benefit for me to accept. Apparently the police had made it clear that they wanted somebody prepared to put in the unsocial hours needed and be available whenever circumstances demanded. I was flattered and jumped at the chance.

I was to be seconded to a Police Traffic Garage and was to undertake no other duties for the foreseeable future.

The officer heading the investigation on the ground was a Pc *Tony Dawson* who was gradually making a name for himself as a HGV specialist. I got on well with him from the start.

I found him very amenable and considering my relative inexperience, which I made no secret of right from the beginning, he seemed quite content to follow my lead throughout the whole operation.

We did a lot of the analytical work from my home which allowed us privacy and avoidance of any possible leaks to the intended company.

We were diligent in our work and by doing a lot of our tasks from my home there was an added bonus for my wife Lin. Not for having me at home so much but for having a good looking bit of '*hot totty*' in the form of a police officer in our house on a regular basis.

It was the only time throughout our marriage that Lin made a comment on another man but it was with justification as he was a striking figure in a conventional way.

After completion of the investigation the operator and many of the drivers were taken before the courts and substantial fines were levied against them for the thousands of offences uncovered.

They were potential killers and companies were thus made aware that they were no longer going to get away with transgressing with impunity.

I learned so much from him about executing search warrants, the actual methodical searching of premises and the putting together of large operations.

This experience served me well sometime later when asked to assist in the searching of premises outside of my sector of a coach company after one of its coaches had been involved in a fatal incident.

We as a Department had instigated the search but without the lead investigator who also happened to be a friend of mine being present after suffering a stroke, the team had started to tread water.

The Area supervisor was in charge and to his credit admitted he had not been involved in the execution of a warrant before and was floundering as how to go about it. I had met him several times on previous occasions and he had even been my boss at one period.

With no wish to embarrass him I surreptitiously asked if he would like me take the lead knowing that if these searches are not performed correctly, any case built against the company could go down the drain.

The knowledge I had gained from *Tony* enabled me to have the confidence to perform this task and as he knew if the case had collapsed it could reflect badly on him.

I know *Tony* felt the same as I did about the knowledge we had gained through each other working together as some years later when it was his sad duty to investigate the killing by a lorry of a Traffic Officer whilst on duty, Tony had tried to get hold of me to assist him in this particularly distressing task.

Unfortunately I was on annual leave and for security reasons only one police officer had my home phone number and whilst he made every effort to contact me it hadn't been possible and so I didn't learn about it until my return.

After the resounding success of the investigation into the transport company *Tony* was given the go ahead by Essex police to continue with the dedicated Major Investigation Task Force throughout the county.

They had obviously come to the conclusion that for morale purposes such a result would ultimately attract other officers into this field which I believe it did.

It was becoming increasingly unnecessary to rely on us 'Mermaids' (The C…S with the Scales) as we were called, due to the fact another of our duties was weighing vehicles.

You can fill in the blanks with either 'HAP' or a rude word 'UNT', it's up to you.

Weighing vehicles was also a power few Police Officers possessed at that time and an overweight vehicle can be just as dangerous as a tired driver or a HGV that is poorly maintained. The combination of over 44 tonnes of sudden death, poor maintenance and a tired driver can be catastrophic, as I witnessed on several occasions.

Shortly after the conclusion of the major transport investigation I was called into see my boss. He informed me that due to the success of that operation the Police were providing the financial resources to proceed jointly with us on another major investigation, this time on a major player in the coach, bus and haulage field.

This was no surprise to me as I previously had dealings with both drivers and the company who always gave me the impression they thought because of the size of the company that they were untouchable and police officers had obviously had the same experience.

They and specifically *Tony* had requested my assistance to once again be seconded full time onto the investigation. I had no wish to offend *Tony* who as I have said I had enjoyed working with but I wanted to get back for a while to normal duties.

The job was varied and interesting but I had been embedded with *Tony* for many months and summer was approaching.

Tony understood and after consultation with my boss it was agreed that I would be available to give advice when necessary but another officer would be the embedded examiner for the investigation as a whole.

MOBILE PHONES

We look upon mobile phones now as an essential part of our everyday lives but back in the late 1980's and 90's they were just a novelty.

One of my bosses actually had one but it bore no relation to the all singing all dancing mini computers most of us now call smart phones.

His was the size of a brick and the battery would last for about half an hour before he needed to plug it in to the mains to recharge. It was easy to criticise him then and he did in all honesty receive a lot of piss taking from most of his colleagues for walking around with this monstrosity.

Not from me though as he was the person who authorised and signed my expense and overtime sheets. He paid for the phone out of his own pocket and this in itself opened him up to ridicule for using it for the Department's business.

In fairness it wasn't long afterwards that the Department issued us with the most up to date new type of mobile phones which were a fraction of the size of the thing he carried around with him.

As a workforce we were mainly against using these new contraptions and were very surprised that the Department had gone to the trouble of spending public money on something that wasn't needed.

They were right and we were wrong as the technology revolution which subsequently followed was to show. Our initial thoughts were that they were a means for management to easily keep track of our movements.

Initially we did not use them and our prehistoric thinking in hindsight was shameful. Personally I didn't know anybody who had a mobile phone and whilst we were given permission to use them privately provide we paid for the calls, the cost of usage to make a call to a landline at the time was astronomical.

At the time all sorts of reasons for not using them were manufactured. They were thought for some time afterwards to be dangerous to a user's health as the radiation they emitted could cause cancer and other dreadful illnesses.

This was new technology and I supposed we viewed it in the same way as our parents must have when television first came into their living rooms after using radio for so many decades.

In our defence though, it could be said that previous experience of the Department's concerns for our health did give us cause for concern.

We were sent on a course somewhere in the wilds near Sellafield Nuclear power plant and along with our colleagues who policed the many vehicles which visited the place, we were shown basic methods on how to detect vehicles which may be emanating harmful radiation.

We were given a Geiger counter and a stick which was about 1 metre long. The idea being that when approaching a suspect vehicle we should touch the vehicle with the stick and put the Geiger counter at the end of it. If the Geiger counter started to crackle we would know immediately that the vehicle was radioactive.

As we charitably explained to the instructor surely we could save the Department money by just approaching the suspect vehicle to within a metre and ask one of our colleagues to confirm if we were turning bright red, thus eliminating the cost of the Geiger counter and the stick.

I kid you not the instructor looked at us as if he was going to cry and said 'but that may kill you'.

As time went on we embraced the phones and even became reliant upon them. There was also a novelty factor to them. I clearly remember going with three or four of my colleagues into a Sainsbury's restaurant to have lunch and being stared at by most of the people in there.

Along with the phones we were provided with leather type holsters which hooked onto our belts to carry them and the size of them was equivalent to a small pistol. The phones were about six inches in length and very few people then had access to them.

Even the police hadn't really started using them yet, so to see four smartly dressed men each with identical holsters caused bewilderment to the feeding customers. It was a revelation to see a whole restaurant of people momentarily and in unison stop eating and talking when one of our phones rang.

To see the phone being answered and spoken into was a sight to behold. Nowadays nobody would even look up but at that time the whole restaurant fell silent.

Most people had never seen a mobile phone in use let alone possess one. To its credit somebody in the Department had the foresight to see the advantages of these new inventions.

Seems madness now but no matter where we went people were fascinated by this new invention and to see their reactions when they were given the opportunity to use it to call somebody they knew was incredible.

To this day my daughters truly think that they introduced me to having a mobile phone but nothing could be further from the truth.

The mind and memory plays tricks on us and the technology has advanced so rapidly that it seems almost impossible to recall the actuality of the past.

TWO DRUNKS ON A COACH

Whilst on patrol with Pc *Noel Simpson* looking for illegal foreign vehicles on a pleasant summer evening in an unmarked Police Traffic car, we decided to park up in the centre roundabout of a junction on the M25 in Essex to look for suspicious foreign HGV's who may have left the motorway to take the A roads to avoid the abundance of Traffic cars patrolling the motorways. A common strategy adopted by mainly foreign vehicles.

We both observed a well liveried coach enter the roundabout and as there seemed nothing suspicious we paid little attention to it.

As we watched the coach did a full circle of the roundabout and we thought little of it. Perhaps the driver had missed the exit he wanted and gone around again. It then did another full circle. To miss the exit once is fine, miss it twice, unprofessional but possible.

To miss it three times something is wrong. In tandem we both looked at each other and nodded. *Noel* put on the blues and two's and off we went in pursuit.

The driver seemed completely oblivious to Noel's attempt to stop him and the reason for it soon became apparent. Once stopped and the doors opened an overwhelming smell of alcohol hit us but this was not unusual for a coach full of day trippers.

It was immediately clear to us both that this driver was in no condition to be in charge of a coach especially one full of passengers. The fumes emanating from him were overpowering and after the formalities *Noel* removed him from the coach to be breathalysed.

I was left with the unenviable task of informing the passengers that the chance of them continuing their journey was unlikely for some considerable time. Apparently they had been on their yearly firm's day out to the coast and the majority of them were worse for wear.

They were so weary that they didn't seem too bothered which was unusual as the level of abuse we were normally subjected to was absent. As I was talking to them a man sleeping in the seat normally kept for a co-driver was beginning to stir and it was evident he was also inebriated.

Once he was fully awake he very quickly became agitated and wanted to know what I was doing on HIS coach.

He was made aware of the situation with regard to the driver currently being breathalysed in the police car and the information appeared to have an immediate sobering effect on him.

When I questioned him with regard to his relationship with the driver he made no attempt to hide the fact that the person *Noel* in fact had in custody was a hitch-hiker he had picked up on the way back from the coast.

He explained that the hitch-hiker had offered to give him relief from driving for a short time to allow the driver to have a short nap as he had consumed quite a lot of alcohol in his time off at the seaside.

The hitch-hiker had told him he had the relevant licence to drive a coach and so the driver in his alcohol infused state had taken the opportunity that had presented itself.

I could see the offences now mounting and put him under caution and informed him that the police officer would now require him also to take a breath test. He started to become irate but by now *Noel* had returned to the coach with the hitch-hiker, who was now under arrest for failing a breath test.

Noel decided that he would call for back-up because regardless of the outcome of the driver's breath test they would both have to be taken into custody for further questioning.

Needless to say the driver also failed the breath test.

We then had the added problem of getting the coach and the by now totally fed up passengers to a safe place to allow them access to toilets and catering facilities. It was decided that I being the holder of a public service vehicle licence would drive the coach to the nearest services on the M25 which was only a few miles away.

This would allow police control to contact the coach company to inform them of the situation and request they arranged for one of their drivers to meet us at the Service Area to allow the coach to continue on its journey.

The company apparently couldn't get anybody there for a few hours so they were informed that I was going to put a Prohibition Notice on the vehicle until such time as the replacement driver arrived. Subject to certain conditions, including relevant checks on the replacement driver's ability to comply with the Drivers Hours Regulations, I would then release the vehicle.

It was decided that the two drunks would be taken to the nearest police station to be processed by *Noel* and that another Traffic car would escort me to the service area where the coach could be left until a replacement driver arrived.

Several hours later *Noel* and I were informed that the replacement driver had arrived at the Services and my presence was required to release the Prohibition Order.

Upon arrival at the services I spoke to him and in doing so noticed that this driver also had a smell of alcohol about him. Further questioning revealed that he had also been drinking before being unexpectedly instructed to go to the service area to retrieve the vehicle.

I informed him that as he hadn't actually taken over control of the coach he wasn't going to be breathalysed and suggested that he contacted his company to see if they had any sober drivers in their employ to enable them to move the vehicle. The cost of parking and feeding the passengers was rapidly rising and I had no doubt that the company would receive many claims for compensation in due course.

A very expensive episode for the company because of the stupidity of one coach driver but miraculously nobody had been hurt.

Both the driver and hitch-hiker were disqualified from driving and I requested that the Traffic Commissioner due to the severity of the offences revoked their Public Service Vehicle Licences.

The consequences of their actions could have been catastrophic.

You couldn't make it up could you?

CHICKEN, CHIPS and ENGINE OIL SIR?

After this episode I didn't think there was much else that could surprise me. I was wrong. The very next day whilst on a multi-agency road check, I was relating the events to colleagues when the police brought in a worn out old Transit van.

They had clearly brought it into the site for our Vehicle Examiners to give it a comprehensive look over. As all of the V.E.'s were tied up with other vehicles I decided to have a chat with the driver. His required documentation seemed to be in order but I was a bit concerned about the weight of the vehicle as it appeared to be sitting on its haunches.

I asked him to open the back doors and immediately wished I hadn't. The sight and smell of the load astonished me. There were dozens if not hundreds of uncooked chickens piled up in the back of the van.

As the vehicle was not refrigerated and there was a spare wheel, a leaking 5 gallon oil can, various tools and a wheel brace and jack perched on top of the mound of dead birds, I assumed he was taking them somewhere to be disposed of.

He seemed completely oblivious to the smells emanating from the van and my thoughts were to try and get him on his way to wherever he was going to dump the birds.

It wasn't to be though. He started to become agitated about the time he was being held up and that his customer was expecting him to have delivered the load at least half an hour previously.

Stupidly I made the mistake of trying to have a joke with him about the chickens wouldn't be bothered as I was delaying their imminent disposal.

Disposal? he cried out !!

He was on his way to a local chicken takeaway and complained bitterly that the owner of the said shop would be furious because they all had to be unloaded and cooked for the evening rush. His late delivery could lose him the contract.

I was way out of my depth but fortunately we had Environmental Health Enforcement Officers on site and thinking nobody would believe what the driver had just told me, I hastily requested their assistance.

They didn't bat an eyelid. Apparently the driver had been stopped several times before for similar offences in other parts of the county and had many prohibition orders placed on him but to no avail.

The business was so lucrative that he just accepted the various fines that had been imposed upon him.

Incredulously they told me that this instance had been a relatively minor offence compared to some their colleagues had encountered.

Where there's muck there's money!

Nothing will change this philosophy. To these criminals public health means nothing. Apparently whilst raiding one set of premises they even found the children of one offender eating the burnt carcass of a rotting animal.

It beggars belief. They just didn't care.

The only answer for these persistent offenders was prison and for any assets they had accumulated from these ill- gotten gains which undoubtedly endangered public health to be seized.

Unfortunately the required laws to enable the authorities to do so did not then exist.

Vehicles with live animals on board were frequently found to be carried in clear breach of environmental health regulations but unless we had the relevant enforcement officers on site to assist us there was little we could do.

POP GOES THE WEASEL

As the two police traffic officers and one of my colleagues were questioning the driver and passenger of an Irish articulated vehicle, they heard what appeared to be a gunshot coming from the back of the trailer.

The vehicle had been brought into a multiple agency road check occurring at a motorway service area on the M25 in Essex and as was customary foreign vehicles were normally directed to a safe area away from other vehicles to allow them to stay in situ should any prohibition orders be placed upon them.

At the time there were not the powers in force to prohibit UK vehicles so they would have been directed to the main site for inspection.

There had been previous instances where vehicles had been found carrying weapons and explosives destined for the I.R.A. which were directly attributable to certain Republic of Ireland hauliers.

The driver and his passenger along with my colleague Keith were led to a place of safety. The vehicle was immediately cordoned off to avoid risks to anybody else. Once away from the immediate vicinity of the vehicle the officers along with many more of their colleagues adopted pre-arranged methods for dealing with this type of situation.

I wasn't on duty on this particular check so what follows can only be a resume of what actually took place as told to me by Keith.

Initially only one noise had been heard and whilst they had no evidence to believe that it was in fact from a gun the officers weren't taking any chances. A senior police officer was about to inform the relevant agencies of the incident when the 'shots' started to increase.

There was by now no doubt there was some kind of explosive device going off inside the trailer. The driver and his passenger had been placed under arrest and held by armed police for questioning by Special Branch Officers upon their arrival at the scene.

Because of the ' Irish troubles' it was standard practice for Scotland Yard's Special Branch to be informed of any activity that we now call acts of terrorism. This was pre 9/11 and the comprehensive anti-terrorism legislation we now have was not then enforced by specific anti-terrorist officers.

The bomb squad had been informed and were in transit but the next sound rendered them surplus to requirements. An almighty flash lit up the whole of the trailer and the container collapsed like a piece of cardboard from the force of the explosion.

Fortunately the actual service area was some distance from the vehicle but nevertheless should there have been time it would have been evacuated. Luckily there were so many police officers on site because of the multi-agency check the area was immediately cordoned off.

Due to the instincts of the original officers who had brought the vehicle into the check and ensured it was positioned as far as possible from any other vehicles, nobody had been hurt.

These men and their colleagues were unsung heroes of the times. They patrolled our busy motorways knowing the dangers they may encounter. Many times the 'troubles' had been brought to the mainland by these hauliers and their complicit drivers.

Whenever a vehicle was stopped they could never be sure that when the door of the cab was opened that they would not be looking down the barrel of an I.R.A. pistol.

The only saving grace was that the drivers generally didn't have suicidal tendencies unlike the modern religious fanatics. Whilst they may not have any scruples about blowing up the population as a whole, they weren't partial to dying themselves.

It wasn't unusual for '*In Memoriam*' business cards with police collar numbers or our names on them in their cabs. It was just intimidation tactics. They were looking to inflict damage on as many people or infrastructures as a whole and not on one police or enforcement officer alone.

The damage caused by the explosion was lessened by the fact that the vehicle had been positioned in such a way whether intentionally or not that it was in a bay surrounded by tall large well established trees and hedgerows and the force of the impact was diminished significantly by them.

To their credit the two officers did not claim to have positioned it thus because of the aforementioned reasons but were pleased they had done so in any case.

However they had no doubt saved many lives because of their professionalism. I had ridden on many occasions with one of them as he enjoyed the ability through my powers to prohibit foreign vehicles.

Together we had the means to hold them for such time to allow us to find an accommodating magistrate to hold a court to deal with them immediately and issue the appropriate fines. They and the vehicle would not be released until the fine had been paid.

British HGV drivers complained bitterly that whilst in continental Europe this frequently happened to them as police on their own had the powers do so, unlike their counterparts in the UK who needed government Traffic Examiners to prohibit vehicles.

Whenever I accompanied Traffic Officers on patrol we had a chance to redress the balance for our drivers. The power of prohibition was subsequently given to authorised police officers and rightly so. It had been an anomaly that had restricted road safety for far too long. They patrolled the roads for 24 hours each day, we didn't.

Amazingly the tractor unit of the vehicle did not catch fire and remained relatively intact. The driver and his passenger who was protesting he was just a hitchhiker were in custody in a cell at a local police station and the forensic teams went about their business at the scene of the incident.

The following is pure conjecture as the security services quite understandably weren't forthcoming with the reasons for the vehicle's presence on this particular stretch of the M25. It had been stopped heading in a southerly direction towards the Queen Elizabeth Bridge so possibly the intention had been to drive onto it and as near as possible to the toll booths on the exit from the bridge and then feign a mechanical breakdown.

After priming the explosive device to allow him time to get well clear, he could casually leave the lorry and walk towards the toll booths as if to summon assistance. Once the trailer exploded there would be instant pandemonium and in the confusion and panic that would ensue he could slip away unnoticed, possibly having a car and driver already waiting on the other side of the booths.

However this could only be pure speculation as the driver would only give 'no comment' answers when interviewed. His passenger however didn't stop talking and would not budge from his story that he had thumbed a lift at South Mimms Service Area and as he had now split from his long term partner he no longer had anything to keep him in the UK so was attempting to reach Dover to catch a ferry and start a new life in France.

His story was consistent and appeared to be plausible unlike the driver who was out and out hard core I.R.A. and proud of it.

Enquiries with the driver's 'employer' in Ireland as expected proved to be fruitless. They spouted the normal well- rehearsed narrative that he was a relatively new driver but had provided all the necessary drivers licence and identification documents before starting employment with them.

They had no idea how his cargo of explosives had gotten on the vehicle, well they wouldn't would they? As the phone conversation with them was going on the Special Branch Officer could see through the window the pigs flying past.

All the owner was interested in was when he was going to get his tractor unit back.

Under P.A.C.E. the normal period of time to interview the driver had been exhausted and as he still had refused to answer any questions a decision had to be made to charge so that he could then be taken to court and be remanded in custody whilst more forensic evidence was gathered, or make application to the court for an extension.

The passenger however was a different matter. Everything he had said appeared to be true and extensive checks with regard to his licence, fingerprints, date of birth and last known address in the UK seemed to be in order.

He was British with no hint of an Irish affiliation or indeed any reason to believe he had any connection to or sympathy with the I.R.A. He had not long split up with his long-time partner, a fact she had corroborated.

He may just have been in the wrong place at the wrong time and it was increasingly beginning to look like that.

Depending on your viewpoint he had been either a very lucky or very unlucky man.

Unlucky in the fact he had hitched with this particular vehicle.

Lucky though that he was still alive and not facing a very long prison sentence.

The same could also be said of the driver. Unlucky that he got caught and was facing a long prison sentence but lucky in the fact that the trailer had exploded accidently in a relatively safe environment. Had it have happened whilst in motion he and probably many others would have been maimed or killed.

A short time later my colleague Keith and I were just leaving a road check when he received a call informing him that Essex Police were about to charge the driver. They were just awaiting a decision from the Crown Prosecution Service regarding the passenger however the feeling was that a court may not grant such an extension as there appeared to be insufficient evidence to link him to the explosion.

Keith had been the original examiner who had placed a prohibition order on the vehicle before it had exploded and he and the police officers had made their timely exit.

The police had requested that he attend the station the two suspects were being held at to enable him to be present when the custody sergeant eventually read out the charges.

There would have been a substantial amount of documentation he also would have to complete to comply with the regulations which would need to be retained as evidence.

The tractor and what was left of the trailer had been taken to a safe holding depot for further forensic examination.

At the time I was using a 'pool car' and as Keith was stationed in another part of the county and the particular police station where the suspects were being held was near to where I lived, I agreed to take him. This would allow him to drop me off afterwards and then take the 'pool car' back to his home on the other side of the county. We would thus be saving the public extra mileage charges. Good Civil Servants were we.

I knew all the custody sergeants there so didn't envisage my presence causing any problems in the custody suite. I had been called out both day and night on numerous occasions to prohibit foreign vehicles for their traffic officers so was familiar with proceedings.

By the time we arrived a decision to release the passenger on police bail had been made by the CPS. It was thought that as he was a British Citizen and as his partner had agreed to allow him to return home for the foreseeable future, this would give him a place of residence to enable him to comply with the bail conditions.

Kenny and I were ushered into the duty Inspector's office where the two original officers who had brought the vehicle into the check and a Special Branch Officer were.

I had met the Special Branch officer on several previous occasions when he had been asked to attend by traffic cops when I had on their behalf prohibited suspicious '*foreign*' vehicles for tachograph offences.

We were brought up to speed as much as was allowed and then waited in the custody suite for the driver and passenger to be brought up from the cells.

The driver was the first to be dealt with and I was sure I had met him before but just couldn't place him. I had met hundreds if not thousands of drivers over the years so it wasn't unusual for me to not be able to identify him.

It couldn't have been at the scene of the explosion as I hadn't been on duty that day. Whilst the charges were being read out to him I searched into the depths of my mind but though sure I had seen him previously it just wouldn't compute.

After the formalities were concluded to which the driver had made no comment he was led back to the cells to await an appearance in court.

The passenger was then brought up to the charge desk to be officially released on police bail, or so he thought. The custody sergeant announced Keith and I as being present and as he glanced around at us his mouth dropped open.

EUREKA!!

It was *Tommy Czerski* and in that instant as he looked pleadingly at me he knew it was over.

It would have been a favour too far.

That's how I knew the driver!

He had been introduced to me at Whittington Hospital some years earlier by *Tommy Czerski* as his partner's nephew.

With a reticent shrug of his shoulders he was returned to the cells for further questioning by Special Branch.

As *Tommy*'s partner was on her way to collect him thinking that he would be going home it wasn't even necessary for a warrant to be issued for her. She would be like a lamb to the slaughter.

They were all purveyors of evil.

Printed in Great Britain
by Amazon

18768974R00161